San Saba Gold

By Richard Willis

San Saba Gold

ISBN: 978-0-9893061-4-0

Richard Willis

ACKNOWLEDGEMENTS

Any attempt to lend historical accuracy to a work of fiction is heavily dependent on the work of others and the assistance of librarians, historians, and others. I am especially indebted to the staff of the Texas Ranger Hall of Fame and Museum in Waco, Texas, the staff of the Eugene C. Barker Texas History Collection at the University of Texas at Austin, and the staff of the Texas State Library and Archives Commission.

The maps were created by slight additons to images provided by Google Earth to whom I am indebted.

My good friend, Barry Starcher provided some editorial help. In addition, he wrote a song, *San Saba Gold*, based on George Dawson's character. You can find his song on the CD entitled *San Saba Gold*.

I am also indebted to my wife, Paula, for her invaluable support and sharp editorial eye.

San Saba Gold

To Paula

Richard Willis

MAPS

San Saba Gold

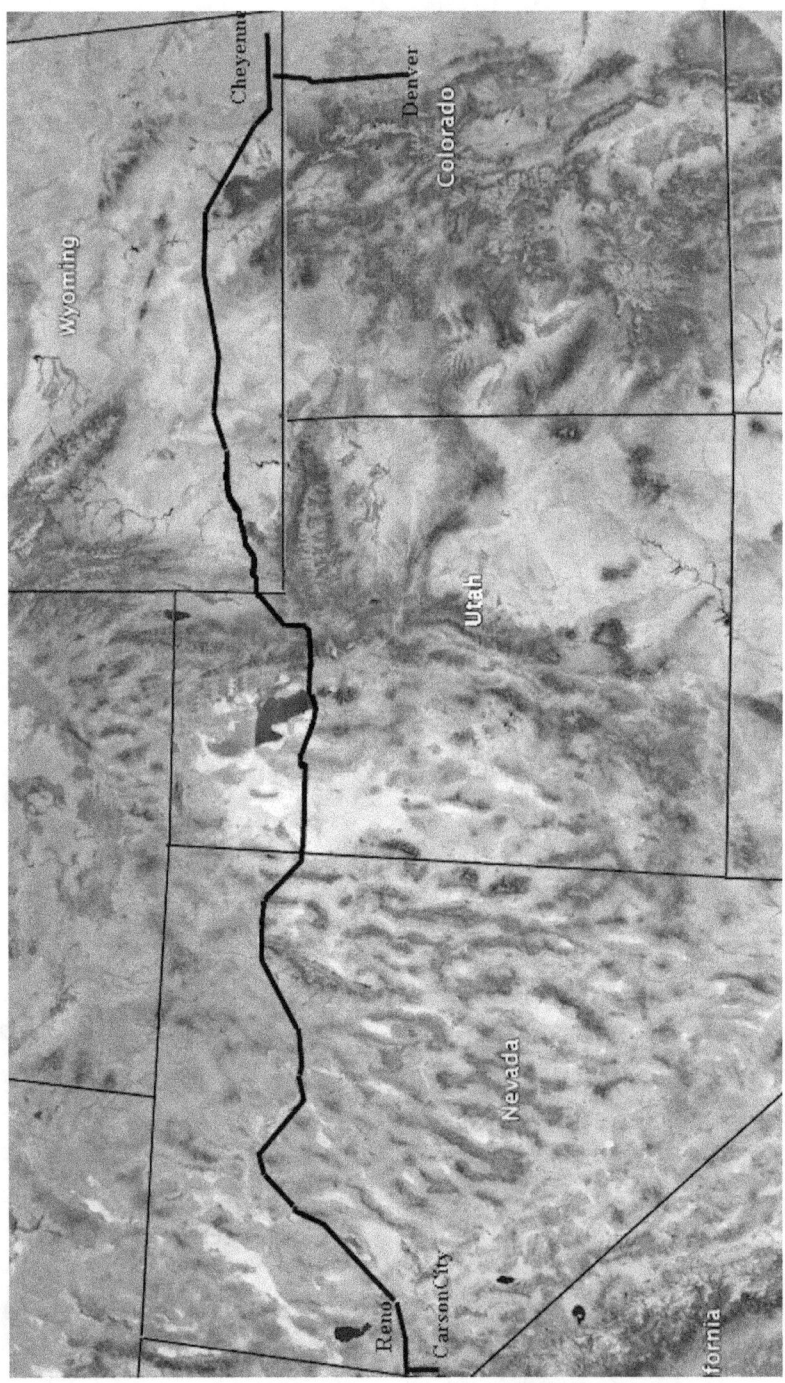

George's Train Route

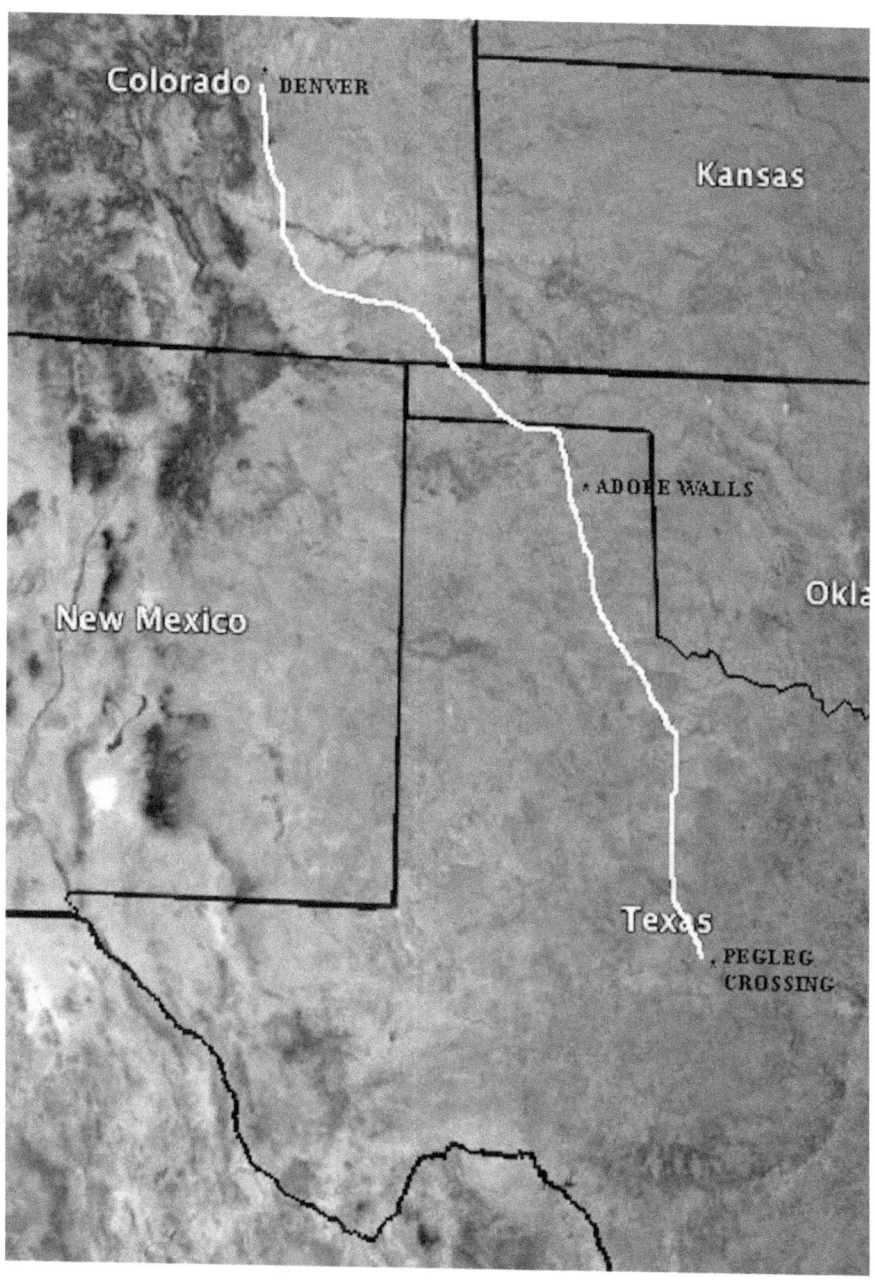

George's Wagon Route

San Saba Gold

J-Bar-H Ranch

GLOSSARY

(My editor suggested that I include a glossary for folks unused to Texan-isms and other western terms.)

Bait of grain – a small portion of grain.

Blue Norther - a cold front marked by a sudden drop in temperature (sometimes up to 25 degrees F within one hour), heavy precipitation, and dark blue-black skies. The phrase originated within Texas.

Caliche – limestone that has broken down to chalky powder. A common soil in the Southwest.

Cedar(s) – Actually they are juniper trees but Southwesterners call them cedars.

Dally – several wraps of a rope (or *riata*) around the saddle horn to serve as an anchor for a roped animal.

Dally Hard And Fast – The end of the rope is tied to the saddle horn rather than just wrapped as in a regular or free dally.

Forty rod – cheap whisky so strong it was said to kill at a distance of forty rods (660 feet).

Grulla –   a horse color. Typically tan-gray or mouse-gray with black mane and tail; legs are usually black and there is often a black stripe down the back.

Huisache – a thorny acacia tree common to south Texas.

Javelina - Peccary, a pig-like animal of northern Mexico and the Southwest U.S.

San Saba Gold

Maverick – term used for unbranded cattle.

Minie ball - a type of muzzle-loading spin-stabilized conical rifle bullet.

Motte – a small stand of trees in an open prairie.

Piggin' string – a leather thong for tying things to a saddle.

Playa – a shallow, flat bottomed lake in a depression mainly in arid plains. These lakes are temporary and appear following heavy rains.

Soogan – Bedroll

Waddies – term often used instead of cowboys.

Whang – see piggin' string.

PROLOGUE

Lieutenant George Dawson's last thoughts were of his wife, Jenny, back home in Illinois. He, a scout, and a dozen troopers were escorting a secret gold shipment to the Federal Arsenal in San Antonio. George felt safe enough about this trip since the one hundred fifty thousand dollars in gold was hidden in the false bottoms of two of the wagons ostensibly loaded with uniforms and saddles destined for the new garrison being built in San Antonio. Except for the sergeants driving the wagons, only he among his troops knew the nature of their mission. It had been necessary to inform the sergeants since any good teamster would detect the extra weight. The Colonel had hand picked the men for the job of driving the wagons.

The bandits struck as the troopers were crossing a ford on the San Saba River deep in central Texas. Dawson's men were outnumbered nearly two to one and severely outgunned. His troopers all had standard issue breech loading Springfields while each bandit had a Henry or a Winchester repeater. The firepower advantage was more like ten to one. George had warned Colonel Morris that this mission required repeaters for his men but Colonel Morris had said that standard issue was better since the mission was secret. Obviously not!

It took less than twenty minutes for the bandits to kill all of the army troopers. As Lieutenant Dawson lay dying in the mud on the south bank of the San Saba, he watched the bandits drive the wagons up the bank and off to the west. They burned the wagon loaded with provisions. Before leaving, they shot arrows into the bodies of his dead men. *Why, shoot arrows into dead men?* he thought. With his last breath, he called out his wife's name.

PART I

Texas Frontier - 1874

I

Early June in the Texas Hill Country is a green time. Wildflowers of every color cover the hillsides. Sergeant Buck McDougal, newly enlisted in the Texas Rangers, sat astride the big paint stallion that he had taken from one of the Comanches he'd killed. He had trailed the Comanches across the Indian Nations, Texas, and Mexico to extract revenge for their murdering his Choctaw grandfather and his cousin and to recover a young woman stolen during the raid. He had been successful in killing his enemies and had rescued the woman down in Mexico. Becky was now on her way home where she would be safe with her family.

A warm humid breeze blew from the southeast as the sun just peaked over the hills to the east. The hillsides were covered in juniper and live oak trees. The Texans called the juniper trees "cedars". Buck rode down a steep hillside toward the valley formed by the Guadalupe River and crossed into the little town of Kerrville, Texas. His orders were to report to Major Jones or the officer in charge at the new Ranger post in or near this town. Buck had met Major Jones in San Antonio as the Major was recruiting for the Frontier Battalion of the newly reconstituted Texas Rangers. Buck declined the offer of a position as Sergeant at the time. However, several weeks later, a Ranger Lieutenant named Jesse Boseman had convinced Buck to enlist.

Buck stopped in town at the livery and learned that the Ranger camp was temporarily located just a few miles west of town. As he rode along the north bank of the Guadalupe, he marveled at the size of the huge bald cypress and pecan trees lining the river. After spending months in the mostly treeless expanses of west Texas and northern Mexico, these trees were awe-inspiring. It was pleasant riding along this beautiful river with no cares except finding the camp. He smelled smoke from cook fires wafting on the breeze before he discovered the camp. The Rangers had located their camp on a tree shaded flat north of the river. He dismounted and walked up to a big tent that he assumed was the officers' quarters.

"Hello," said Buck to a young sandy-haired man wearing a fork-tailed coat and standing at the front of the tent. "I'm Buck McDougal. I was enlisted in Laredo by Lieutenant Boseman who's with McNelly's Battalion. I was told to report here for duty."

"Howdy," said the young Ranger. "My name's Johnny Wilkins. Pleased to meet ya. Captain Coldwell's gone to Austin with Lieutenant Nelson to meet with Major Jones and the other Captains. Lieutenant Dolan's in charge but he's out on a scout up Johnson Creek. A rancher lost a few head of stock and said that the rustlers' ponies were unshod. Sounds like Injun sign to me. Anyhow, why don't you go talk with Sergeant Jones? That's him settin' on that lard bucket over yonder by that big pecan tree fishin'. He'll assign you to a tent and such."

Prior to the Civil War, the Texas Rangers had driven most of the hostile Indians out of central and eastern Texas. During the Civil War, the Rangers had been incorporated into the Confederate Army and deployed east out of Texas. Following the war, the Union government took control of governing the state and disbanded the Rangers. The Union Army saw no need to protect the Texans at the western edge of settlement. Therefore, the Texas frontier lay unprotected. The Comanches and Kiowas responded by raiding south and east out of their strongholds in Palo Duro Canyon and the Indian Nations. The Kickapoos and Lipan Apaches swarmed up from Mexico on raids as well. As a result, the white frontier was pushed eastward more than one hundred miles.

In 1874 after years of 'Reconstruction', democracy returned to Texas. The newly elected legislature and newly elected Governor Coke moved to re-establish a protective force to regain control of the western frontier. The Texas Rangers were reconstituted. The Frontier Battalion was assigned to form a line from the Brazos to the Nueces Rivers. Concurrently, an additional company, named the Special Force under Captain McNelly, was positioned in the area between Brownsville and Laredo to protect the Rio Grande border from the constant raiding of both white and Mexican bandits.

The Frontier Battalion was placed under the able leadership of Major John Jones. Major Jones was only five feet eight inches tall and weighed barely one hundred thirty-five pounds but his commanding presence made him big in the eyes of friend and foe alike. Major Jones established six companies designated A through F and stationed them in a north to south line. Company F, the southernmost, was mustered in Kerrville and later headquartered about twenty-fives miles southwest in order to provide protection in the large area between the headwaters of the Nueces and Llano Rivers. Captain Neal Coldwell and his two Lieutenants, Pat Dolan and F.W. Nelson, commanded Company F.

The Rangers, themselves, were mostly single young men of frontier stock. They were required to supply their own tack and a good horse. The state provided a .50 caliber Sharps breech loading carbine and a side arm, although many of the Rangers preferred to use their own weapons. The state also provided food, such as it was, a piece of ground to sleep on, forage for the horses and ammunition for the state provided weapons.

Rangers who used their own weapons were responsible for ammunition. Occasionally the men were paid, but the pay was sporadic and often they went unpaid. Also, if they received weapons from the state, the cost was deducted from their pay.

San Saba Gold

Although the Rangers were, in essence, a military force, they wore no uniforms and followed only the most casual of military demeanor. Men signed on for varying terms of service, rarely more than one year. Recruits were screened for their moral character, hardiness, horsemanship, and marksmanship.

During the period just following the Civil War, Texas filled with outlaws and disgruntled former Union and Confederate soldiers. Hostile Indians ranged the frontier, feuds flared between groups with sympathies on both sides of the Civil War. Cutthroats and bandits roamed freely. The Rangers were given the responsibility of bringing order to the land. The Federal troops stationed in Texas had, so far, provided little relief. One advantage given to the Rangers was that their jurisdiction covered the entire state. Local and county boundaries did not limit them.

Buck led the big paint stallion down to the riverbank and tied the reins to a low branch on one of the huge cypress trees. The horse began to drink from the crystal clear water running a foot deep over the snow-white limestone bottom. The water deepened just up stream where Sergeant Jones was fishing. Here the river darkened to a deep green.

Sergeant Jones was wearing a worn cotton shirt under a black leather vest. He had a large Mexican sombrero on his head of curly red hair. "Havin' any luck?" asked Buck as he walked up behind the fisherman.

"Naw, jist drownin' grasshoppers," said the Sergeant. "Lawdy, you're a big 'un."

Buck was an imposing figure. Half Choctaw and half Scots-Irish, he stood six feet two inches tall and weighed a solid one hundred ninety-five pounds. He was wearing a buckskin shirt and pants that were covered in dried blood. He held a wide-brimmed floppy leather hat in his left hand. A Smith and Wesson revolver was holstered on his hip and a cap-and-ball Colt was stuck in his belt. His shiny black hair fell to his shoulders, but besides his size, his deep blue eyes were the first thing someone noticed.

Sergeant Jones continued, "Who're you?"

"I'm Caleb McDougal, but ever'body calls me Buck. Here's my enlistment papers."

"Sez here you were signed up by Boseman down in Laredo and detailed to us as a sergeant," Sergeant Jones said as he looked up from the paper Buck had handed to him. "Lawdy, are you hurt? Your britches and shirt's covered up in dried blood and it looks like there's a hole there on your left side."

"Most of the blood is from my horse," said Buck. "Comanches killed him in the brush down south of here. One of 'em put an arrow through my side here but it sailed on through without touchin' my vitals. I put a mud dauber and cactus poultice on it and it's healin' up okay."

"Since you're here and ridin' a Comanche pony, I reckon you got the Comanches."

"Yep, I chased them clear across the Nations and down the Pecos into Mexico before I caught 'em back up here in Texas near Frio Town. They killed some of my kin and stole a woman. Maybe you heard of the leader, White Elk? One of those scalps tied to my pony is his."

"Yeah, I heard of him. He's been raisin' havoc ever since the big fight with Kit Carson at Adobe Walls. How about the woman? Did you find her?"

"Yep, she got sold to some grandee down in Mexico. I caught up with them and got her back. I left her with an ex-Ranger friend name of Cal Watson. He promised to take her to San Antonio and put her on the stage back to her family. I left her with Cal because I was still after the Comanches."

"Why, I knowed Cal back afore the war. We rangered together for a spell. Last I heard, he was runnin' a store down on the border. Let's git you settled in. That third tent over yonder is empty now. Why don't you stow your gear in there? I'll see you at chuck tonight."

"Once I unload a few things into the tent, I want to ride back to town and buy a new shirt and a few other things, if that's okay."

"Have at it, jist be back before sundown fer roll call. Oh, and the Major is pretty set on horse color for us Rangers. That paint pony of yours'll never pass muster. Best trade him for a black or a bay or a roan in town. And, the Major don't allow no mares. He says that they cause trouble betixt the stallions and mares go to foalin' just when you're on a long scout. If'n I was you, I'd get me a gelding. Easier to manage. Besides, the Major ain't real keen on stallions, neither."

Buck decided to keep the paint. He had started calling him Patch. But, rules were rules, so he bought a bay gelding from the man running the livery. He bought a sturdy pair of brown pants and two cotton shirts. He stopped in at the barbershop for a bath, a haircut, and a shave.

Late that afternoon, he rode back to camp on the bay leading Patch. Of course, he would be expected to provide for the feed that Patch ate. He spent the evening meeting the other Rangers in camp.

Buck had two squads of fifteen young men assigned to him. He spent the next two days interviewing them and testing their shooting and riding skills. He selected two to serve as his Corporals and took the names to Lieutenant Dolan for approval.

"I like your choices, Buck. These men are from fine families and have the skills we need to head up your squads. I received a letter from Major Jones about you. He is mighty pleased with that herd of horses that you recovered from the Comanches and sent to Uvalde. Half of them had registered brands, so they got returned to their owners but the rest were sold and the money added to the Ranger appropriation."

II

One morning an exhausted boy stumbled into camp. The boy's homespun shirt was torn and his face and arms were bleeding from numerous scratches. He had obviously been running through the brush. Buck happened to be standing outside Sergeant Jones' tent as the boy flopped down in the dirt gasping for breath. Buck gave him some water and asked, "What can we do for you, young feller?"

The boy gasped, "Me and Paw was headin' back to our ranch from town when a bunch of bandits stolt our wagon and kilt Paw. I hid in the bresh until they left. I knowed you Rangers was camped here, so I run all the way."

Buck stuck his head into the tent and said, "Jones, you may want to hear this."

Sergeant Jones crawled out of his tent and asked, "What's this all about?"

Buck turned to the boy and said, "Okay, young feller, what's your name and tell us your tale from the beginning."

"Well, sir, it ain't no tale, it's the gospel. My name is Tommy Womack and me and Paw had come down from our ranch to get some supplies in town. We was on our way home when these four fellers swarmed us. They said for us to git down offen the wagon or they'd kill us. Paw grabbed up his scattergun what was under the seat but one of them outlaws shot him dead. I jumped off the wagon and dived into the bresh along side of the road. One of them fellers hopped onto the wagon and they all drove off north towards the Per'enales. Soon as they was around the bend, I come a-runnin' to your camp."

Buck asked, "How far north did this happen?"

Tommy replied, "Couldn't a-been more'n a couple miles since I ran straight here."

Buck asked, "What did these outlaws look like?"

Tommy replied, "They had their neckerchiefs pulled up over their faces so I couldn't tell much. The one who shot Paw was kinda small and he had red hair. I was too busy getting' away to git a good look at the others. The red-head was ridin' a blue roan."

Sergeant Jones said, "Buck, get four or five of your men and ride out to see if you can catch these killers."

Four of Buck's men were sitting on the ground in the shade of a big pecan tree playing cards. Buck walked up and said, "Saddle up, boys, we've got some bad outlaws to catch. Be ready in ten minutes. Bring enough provisions for two to three days and bring a shovel. We've got a man to bury."

Buck grabbed his guns and ran to the remuda. He saddled his gelding and a small black for Tommy Womack. He called to the boy who was eating pinto beans off of a tin plate while squatting next to the cook's campfire, "Tommy, finish up your *frijoles* and climb up on this black. I want you to join us so that you can show where the attack took place."

An hour later, they found Mr. Womack lying dead along side of the road. Buck said, "Nate, you and Zeke take this boy to his home and bury this feller wherever Tommy's Momma tells you. Once you're done with the buryin', come a-runnin'. I'll leave sign so's you can catch up to us. Jim and Bill, let's follow these wagon tracks and see what we can find."

The tracks left the road and led west up a little valley covered in tall blue stem grass and with a few live oaks scattered about. As the Rangers topped a little rise, Jim Baker called out, "Look yonder by them cedar trees. I think it's the wagon."

One of the wagon's wheels had come off due to a loose

hub nut. Rather than search for the missing hub nut and make the simple repair, the outlaws had abandoned the wagon. A quick check revealed that the wagon had little of value to the bandits. Although they could have taken things of which the Rangers were unaware. A scout of the trail beyond the wagon revealed four sets of hoof prints heading west.

When it got too dark to follow the tracks, Buck called a halt. "Boys, we might as well make cold camp here and let Nate and Zeke catch up. I'd rather not stumble on the bandits in the dark when we're outnumbered. I'll stand first watch. Get yourselves a little jerky and a biscuit to eat and then get some sleep. No fire and no smoking, I don't want the outlaws to see that we are following."

Nate and Zeke drifted in late that night. The Rangers were in the saddle at first light. Buck led out scanning the ground for tracks.

Suddenly, Jim gave a low whistle and said, "Buck, I think I smell coffee."

Buck said, "I smell it now, too, and cedar wood smoke. The breeze has shifted out of the southwest during the night. Nate, take my reins and lead my pony. Y'all wait a few minutes while I slip off upwind and see if I can see who's makin' breakfast."

Buck scrambled over a low ridge and peeked down on a campsite. The blue roan and three bay geldings were picketed between two Spanish Oak trees. Buck eased back down the ridge a bit and whistled a quail hen 'come covey' call to his men. Off in the distance, Jim answered with a clear 'Bob White'. The Rangers tied their horses well back from the ridge and hastened up to where Buck sat.

Buck said, "The owl hoots are just down the other side of the ridge. Best I can make out, three of them are still in their soogans and 'Red' is rustlin' up breakfast. Zeke and Nate, you fellers ease off to the south and try to slide around to the west of 'em. Jim, you come at them from the south and, Bill, you take the north. I'll come down on them from the ridge. Don't shoot each other and wait until I give them a chance to surrender. If they put up a fight, have at 'em."

As planned, Buck waited fifteen minutes before easing down the slope toward the outlaws' camp. Steam was escaping from the spout of a coffee pot where it sat bubbling on a rock at the edge of the fire. Red and one of the other men were cooking strips of bacon wrapped on the ends of sticks. When he was about twenty feet away, Buck stepped out from behind a cedar, leveled his rifle toward the two men and said, "Stand up and keep your hands away from your shooters. You are surrounded by Texas Rangers and are under arrest."

Red and the other man stood up and held their hands up at shoulder level. Suddenly a pistol cracked from the direction of the two men in their bedrolls followed quickly by a yelp. As Buck turned to see what was happening, Red reached for his revolver. Before he could clear the gun from the holster, Zeke's Winchester banged and Red fell face down into the fire. "Use your left hand and throw your shooter over here by me," Buck said to the other bandit. "Grab Red by the legs and pull him out of the fire. If'n you don't want to get shot, keep your hands away from Red's gun."

Meanwhile, the other four Rangers had converged on the two men in their bedrolls. One of the men was moaning. "Jim, come keep an eye on this *hombre*," said Buck. "What's the matter with the moaner?"

"Looks like he done shot himself in the leg," said Nate. "I reckon he tried to yank his revolver from inside his soogan."

"Get 'em up. Take that rope from the saddle over there and tie 'em to that oak tree," said Buck.

The youngest outlaw said, "Y'all ain't gonna hang us, are you?"

Buck smiled and said, "Not unless you cause us any more trouble."

★★★

Buck filed his report with Lieutenant Dolan and went to his tent to rest. The killer, Red, was dead and the other three were locked up in the Kerrville jail awaiting trial. The Womack's wagon wheel hub nut had been found and a quick repair made. The wagon and most of its contents were returned to the Womack family. The outlaws had used only part of a slab of bacon and some coffee. A small keg of black powder and some lead bars for bullet making were recovered from the outlaw camp. Their horses were added to the Ranger remuda.

Buck stretched out on his cot and tried to sleep but he was restless. *What am I doin' huntin' outlaws and spending my time drillin' these Rangers?* he thought. *I'm signed on for at least a year and I ought to be on my way home to see about Becky.* He drifted off to a troubled sleep.

San Saba Gold

III

Becky, a full-blood Choctaw, had endured the hardships of capture by the Comanches and the long ride across Texas and northern Mexico. The Comanches had sold her to Quintana Gomez, a wealthy Mexican Comanchero. Quintana took her to his ranch in Mexico where he sold her to a man named *Señor* Ortega to serve as a nanny for his grandchild. Buck had trailed her all the way from his family store in the Indian Nations where the Comanches had murdered her husband, Buck's cousin, during the raid. Buck rescued her as *Señor* Ortega was taking her to Chihuahua City. Buck brought her out of Mexico. She was now sitting on the wagon seat next to Cal Watson, a former Ranger, who had promised Buck to take her to San Antonio so that she could return to her family in the Indian Nations. They had left Cal's store in San Felipe del Rio two days earlier.

"I wonder if Buck has caught up to the Comanches yet and if he's safe," said Becky.

Cal replied, "Now don't you be a-worryin' about Ol' Buck. He rode halfway to blazes and gone to fetch you and whupped Quintana Gomez and his boys along the way. Plus, you tolt me that he and his Lipan pardner, Angry, kilt near to half of them Comanches up on the Pecos whilst they was trailin' you. I 'spect Buck'll do all right. You can tell by the fire in his eyes that he's *mucho hombre.*"

"I know that," said Becky, "and I know that he's safe. I can feel it somehow. Just like I could feel that he was following us down from the Nations. It's just that everything is so jumbled up. I don't know whether to cry or laugh or cuss. Buck and I had feelings for each other before I married his cousin, James. Now, I just don't know."

"I'd let it fester awhile. Just give things some time. You and Buck are young and got lots of time to sort things out. Get yourself back home and spend some time with your folks. I know from my Rangerin' days that it takes a man time to settle down after he's been in a fight. Your Buck will need some time after he's kilt his enemies."

They jolted along the dusty road without talking until nearly sunset. "Uvalde's just a few miles east of us," said Cal. "We'll go ahead and cross the Nueces and spend the night in town. I don't know about you but I'd just as soon not sleep on the ground again. We'll get us a couple of rooms at the hotel. It's near to three days to San Antone from here so a good night's sleep will be the last we'll see of beds for a while. When we get to San Antone, I'll take you to the Mercado where you can shop for clothes and whatever else you need for your trip home."

Two days after arriving, Becky left San Antonio aboard the stagecoach to Austin. That morning, she sent a telegraph message to her parents informing them that she was safe and would be home in a week or so. Cal had seen her off at mid-day before returning to his home in San Felipe del Rio.

Becky's fellow travelers included a beefy man in his fifties who said he was a Circuit Judge; a scruffy looking man named Jake; and a young woman named Sally Greenville who said she was off to visit her Aunt May in Austin. Even though it was early June, it was already hot. The chalky caliche dust kicked up by the team and coach wheels poured in through the coach windows as they rocked and bounced along the rough road.

Late that afternoon, they arrived in New Braunfels for an overnight stop. The driver had explained that the stage no longer ran at night due to the frequent robberies on the road to Austin.

New Braunfels was a new experience for Becky. The locals were mostly Germans who had emigrated from Europe in the 1840's. The food was good though a bit different from what she was accustomed. The music playing at a social club next to the hotel was lively. The men and women were dancing a lively step they called the polka. Becky and Sally edged into the dancehall and found seats near a window. Their entrance had not gone unnoticed by a number of young men in the room.

After an early breakfast, they re-boarded the coach and set out for Austin. Sally said, "Lordy, but my feet ache. I never danced so much in my life. I'm glad that you grabbed me at ten o'clock so we could get back to the hotel and our room."

"My feet hurt, too," said Becky. "I think that fellow named Hans would have asked you to marry him if we stayed one more day." Both of them giggled as Sally grinned.

"He is a farmer and I grew up on a farm," said Sally. "Farmers work themselves and their wives to death. I don't plan to be a farm wife."

"Well, he seemed nice enough and he sure was good looking," said Becky.

Sally nudged Becky in the ribs with an elbow and said, "What about you and that Gunter? He sure was swingin' you around the floor. He was lookin' at you like you were a big old slice of peach pie."

They continued their banter as the coach jolted along. It was a bit cooler this morning and looked like it would rain before the day was out. They briefly stopped at an inn in San Marcos for an early lunch before continuing towards Austin. At mid-afternoon the coach lurched to a stop. Becky stuck her head out of the window and saw three men blocking the road. They had their rifles aimed at the driver and all had bandanas pulled up across their faces.

One of the men fired his rifle into the air and shouted, "You there, stick your head back inside a-fore I blow it off."

Becky ducked back inside and said, "I think we are being robbed."

The scruffy passenger named Jake pulled his pistol and said, "That's right, ladies, give me your purses. Judge, I'll take that pistol in your coat pocket and your wallet. The watch, too, if you don't mind."

Becky thought, *I'll be damned if I'm going to give this crook my travel money after all I've been through.* She passed Sally's purse to the bandit and, while the Judge was fishing his wallet and pistol out of his coat, Becky hurled herself onto Jake and knocked his pistol out of the coach window. A well-placed knee to the groin had taken the fight out of Jake. Before he could recover, the Judge had picked up his own pistol and now had Jake covered. Becky grabbed Sally's purse off of the seat next to Jake and returned to her own seat.

"What the hell's goin' on in there, Jake?" asked one of the highwaymen. "You got their money yet?"

Judge Magee said quietly, "Jake, if that is your name, what you say next will determine if you live or die right here."

"I'll be just a minute, Pete," shouted Jake. "Y'all stay there watchin' the driver."

Pete shouted, "Jake, there's riders comin' up the road at a gallop. We're pullin' out." The robbers mounted their horses, rode west, and disappeared into a cedar thicket.

Judge Magee said, "Jake, ease open the door and step out of the coach. Try anything funny and I'll blow you to Kingdom Come."

Jake opened the door and stepped out just as two men rode up to the coach. One of the riders said, "I'm Sheriff Zach Bugg, and this here's Paul Johnston with the Pinkerton's. What's going on here?"

Judge Magee stepped out of the coach and said, "Howdy, Zach, four fellows tried to hold us up. Three of them rode west into the brush when you showed up. This Jaybird was part of their gang."

Sheriff Bugg said to the driver, "Sam, y'all are still well inside Hays County and my jurisdiction. I'd appreciate it if you'd tie up this feller and haul him back to San Marcos. Have my Deputy lock him in a cell. Me and Mr. Johnston will light out after the other three."

Sam said, "This'll sure blow my schedule all to sunders. Liable to get me fired."

Sheriff Bugg said, "Don't worry about that, I'll talk to the stage line when I get back and explain what happened. They'll be tickled that you didn't lose the strongbox nor have your passengers robbed. And, Judge Magee can vouch that I ordered you back to San Marcos."

Sheriff Bugg and the Pinkerton man wheeled their horses about and galloped off on the trail of the hold-up men.

The stagecoach stopped in front of the jailhouse. The driver said, "Judge, let's get this outlaw locked up. We don't have near enough daylight left to make it to Austin today. I'll send a wire and let 'em know we'll be there afore noon tomorrow. Ladies, I'll drop you off at the inn where we was at noon today. Tell 'em to give you a room and charge it to Sheriff Bugg's account. We'll leave early in the morning, so get your breakfast early and be ready to leave."

San Marcos was a sleepy little village where most of the folks spoke Spanish. Sally and Becky checked into the inn and then took a stroll around the town square. There wasn't much to see. A few clapboard buildings and a stone jailhouse lined the square. The center of the square was mostly bare caliche with two medium-sized live oaks and a couple of wooden benches. Two old geezers were napping on one of the benches.

That night Becky lay in her bed and thought about the events of the past year. The sound of a guitar and someone singing a Spanish song came to her through the open window.

The only words that she could hear distinctly enough and understand were *Mi corazón. My heart,* she thought, *what is in my heart? James was murdered, Buck is God knows where, and I'm heading home to what? Momma and Papa, of course, but then what?* She finally drifted into a fitful sleep.

Becky felt like she had barely gotten to sleep when Sally was pecking at the door and calling her name. She peeked toward the window and saw that it was just getting light to the east. "I'm up," she yelled toward the door, even though she wasn't. She arose and let Sally in.

"You best get a move on," admonished Sally, "or you'll miss breakfast. If I know that stage driver, he'll be pulling up out front before you know it. I'll see you downstairs, sleepyhead."

They reached Austin at midday and enjoyed lunch at a small café near the railroad station. Then, Sally and Becky did a bit of shopping and marveled at the buildings, especially the State Capitol. After an hour or two of strolling up and down the main street of Austin, Becky went to the railway station to buy her ticket for the train east.

IV

Early summer is hot and humid in south central Texas. Buck and his men made numerous, exhausting scouts to the headwaters of the Guadalupe, Nueces, and Llano rivers looking for Indian sign. They found little evidence of activity. Buck decided that they were wearing out themselves and their horses for nothing. *The Comanches, Kiowas, Kickapoos, and Lipans got more sense than to raid when it's this derned hot,* thought Buck. But, orders were orders.

Major Jones had arrived on his routine inspection tour with news of a big battle with Comanches, Kiowas, and Cheyennes up at Adobe Walls in the Panhandle. According to him, a group of up to one thousand hostiles had attacked some buffalo hunters who were camped there. Three of the hunters, who were outside the camp, were killed but the hunters inside the thick adobe structure held off the Indians with their heavy buffalo guns and drove them away. Billy Dixon borrowed another hunter's .50-90 Sharps and made a shot of over one mile knocking down an Indian sitting on a horse next to war chief Quanah Parker. That effectively ended the siege. The Indians decided that their 'Medicine' had turned bad. So, they left.

As Buck walked up to Captain Coldwell's tent, Major Jones stood and said, "Why, hello again. Buck, isn't it?'

"Yessir," replied Buck. "It's good to see you again. As you can see, I took your advice and joined."

"I thought that was your name on the enlistment roster that Pat Dolan sent to me last month. Good to have you with us."

★★★

San Saba Gold

After Buck walked away from the officer's tent, Major Jones said to Captain Coldwell, "I liked that man the first time I saw him on the Plaza in San Antonio. Can you spare him? I need a steady man with me. I've put together an escort by drawing a few men from each company but I need another steady man. You've got three sergeants including him while most of the companies have only two. I know that you got him as a bit of a surprise anyway. Of course, I can order him to my staff but I want you to have a say."

Coldwell replied, "He is a fine Ranger and if half of his story about his chase of the Comanches across Texas is true, then he is a prize indeed. But the fact is that I can do without him if you need him. Just give him back if you decide that you don't need him anymore. The other Captains can find their own prizes!"

"Thanks," laughed Major Jones. "I'll cut the order to read that Sergeant McDougal of Company F is 'temporarily' detailed to join my escort. We'll leave in the morning for Menardville and Captain Perry's Company D headquarters. If any messages arrive for me after we leave, send a courier to Menardville."

Buck stretched out on his cot and listened to the night sounds. The camp had settled down for the night. He could hear snoring from some of the men, cicadas and katydids buzzing and chirping in the trees, frogs croaking along the riverbank, an owl hooting off downriver somewhere, and coyotes yodeling up on the hillside to the north. He was bone tired but too tired to sleep. The cot was more comfortable than the ground but not by much and the cot was too damned short. His feet hung over the end. As he gazed up at the underside of the tent above him, he thought of Becky. Surely, she was back home now safe with her folks. *I need to write her a letter,* Buck thought. *James ain't been dead but a few*

months and she needs time to sort out her grievin' and get over her bein' taken by the Comanches. I'll tell her that I'll give her a while afore I discuss any future for us.

Buck awoke with a start. As he shook the fog out of his mind, he realized that the clatter of someone cooking was what had awakened him. His stomach barked for food. He pulled on his boots, slapped his hat on his head, and strode out of the tent. Major Jones and Captain Coldwell were standing near the cook fire drinking coffee while one of the privates was making breakfast for them. *Major Jones always looks like he's dressed to go to a weddin',* thought Buck. *I don't know how he can always look so tidy out here in the dirt with the rest of us.*

"Buck," said Captain Coldwell, "you're being temporarily reassigned to serve as part of Major Jones' escort. After breakfast, gather your gear, saddle your pony, and report to Major Jones' tent. You can leave your paint in the remuda. We'll watch over him and remember whatever grain he gets will come out of your wages. He's your pet not a Ranger horse."

"Yes, sir, take good care of him," said Buck. "He's more horse than any of the rest of these mounts, but I'll not use him when I'm on duty. Regulations, you know." Buck winked at the Captain and nodded toward the Major's back.

Major Jones stopped and without turning said, "I hear you, Buck, but I can't have Rangers riding around on horses that are obviously Comanche ponies. Half the civilians don't trust us as is."

Buck whispered to Captain Coldwell, "Lordy, he's got the ears of a cat. I didn't reckon he could hear me."

Coldwell whispered back, "He can see out of the back of his head, too."

An hour later, Buck sat on his horse waiting for Major Jones to give the order to move out. They formed a double column of twenty Rangers with Major Jones in the lead and four out riders a few hundred yards to either side of the column. Two men were out in front serving as an advance guard and looking for suspicious tracks.

Sergeant Brown rode next to Buck directly behind the Major. Sergeant Brown said to Buck, "The Major don't tell us much about where he's takin' us but after bein' with him awhile, you can make a fair guess based on the direction he heads and how much grub was packed on the mules. I figger we're headin' for Menardville based on the direction and the load on the mules."

The trip to Menardville was uneventful. After a few days at the camp of Company D, Major Jones and his escort headed north to Company B where Indians had stolen horses and killed a man on the Loving Ranch. Lieutenant Wilson came out of Major Jones' tent and walked over to where Buck and three other Rangers were sitting. He said to Buck, "Sergeant, pick five men and prepare for a two day scout. Meet me over by that live oak in thirty minutes."

"Yes, sir," replied Buck.

The next morning they were riding along Salt Creek with Buck out front. He lifted his fist in the 'Stop' signal and rode back to the others. "Lieutenant, I think you had better come take a look at the tracks I found. It looks like a large party of unshod horses crossed the creek just ahead."

They rode ahead and dismounted. "Could be a herd of mustangs," said Lieutenant Wilson.

"That's what I thought at first," said Buck, "but look here where this pony climbed the bank. He had a rider or he would not have slid back like that. And, over here by that yucca plant, a man wearing moccasins dismounted and relieved himself."

"Let's hurry back to camp and report this to the Major. How old do you think these tracks are?"

Buck said, "Those horse droppings over there are still wet and warm. I'd say less than an hour."

They returned to their group of Rangers and then rode

hard back to Company B headquarters. After hearing the lieutenant's report, Major Jones' said, "Lieutenant, take thirty or so men from the escort and Company B and get hot after that trail. I'll take Sergeant McDougal and the rest of the escort with me. As soon as we can get the rest of the men mounted and provisioned, we'll follow up behind you."

Two hours later, Brownie Smith called out, "There's two of them just ahead. Let's get 'em, boys."

Most of the advance guard charged ahead hot on the heels of the fleeing Kiowas. As they entered Lost Valley, Indians began shooting from hiding places in the brush and rocks on the hillsides. "Laws," shouted Johnny Black, "there's a hundred of them or more! We're in a trap."

By that time the full escort was under fire and trapped in the middle of the valley. Very quickly, two Rangers were killed and two more wounded. The Rangers dismounted and took what cover they could find.

Major Jones shouted from his hiding spot, "Men, they've got us outnumbered three or four to one. We're trapped here without enough water and no way to get everybody out. I need a volunteer to ride to Fort Richardson at Jacksboro for help."

"I'll go," said Buck, "but my horse is worn down and I don't know the way to Jacksboro."

Lee Corn, one of the wounded Rangers, spoke up, "Take my horse. He's a fast one and if'n you give him his head, he run straight for Jacksboro. That's home for him and where he'll expect to be fed."

"Okay," said Buck. He leapt into the saddle, crouched low, and dashed off to the east in a hail of bullets.

"He got clear," said Lieutenant Wilson, "I saw him top that far ridge."

Shots were exchanged for several more hours and many of the Rangers' horses were killed or crippled. The late afternoon sun was brutal. The temperature was at least one hundred degrees. Two hours passed without a shot being fired. Grasshoppers were ratcheting in the brush and cicadas buzzed from every tree. Biting flies plagued the men hiding in the dirt behind whatever rock, bush, or tree they had used for cover.

Finally, Major Jones stood up and said, "Boys, I believe the Indians have left. We need to collect our dead and move our wounded to someplace where they can receive adequate treatment."

Sergeant Brown spoke up, "Major, the Loving ranch house ain't but a few miles off. That'd be the closest place for help."

"Catch up your horses, men," said Major Jones. "Put the wounded on horseback. Tie them on if need be. Any of those wounded horses that look too injured to recover need to be put down. A couple of you men see to it. Gather up the tack from the dead horses and tie it onto a few of the unwounded horses. Those of us without mounts will walk. Sergeant, lead the way. Corporal Smith, you ride on ahead and alert the Lovings that we are coming and have injured men."

In the dark of the early morning hours, Buck and two companies of the U.S. 10th Cavalry arrived at the ranch. Jim Loving's ranch foreman had sent one of his ranch hands to intercept the soldiers and lead them back to the ranch.

The Cavalry officers and Major Jones met and planned a return to the site of the battle. After daylight, the Rangers and the U.S. soldiers scouted the valley where they determined that the Indians had indeed left the area.

V

After waving goodbye to Sally from the coach window, Becky draped a new yellow shawl over her shoulders. She had purchased it in Austin for the train trip. The light fabric was comfortable as well as good looking. She was wearing the bright yellow dress given to her by the wife of the Comanchero to whom she had been sold by the Comanches. The memories were unpleasant but the dress was pretty and she liked it. She also wore a bonnet to shield her face from the sun. Her skin was dark enough already and she saw no benefit in turning darker. At least, not until she got home.

The train lurched forward with a bang and a rattle as the locomotive chuffed and hissed. Smoke from the engine wafted through the open windows of the car. This was Becky's first train ride and she was excited but tried not to show it. After a little while, the Conductor came through the car punching tickets. As he got to Becky, she said, "This thing is flying along. How fast do you think we are going?"

The Conductor replied, "Ma'am, this here train hits thirty miles an hour or better dependin' on the slope and whether she's roundin' curves or not. Just sit back and enjoy the ride. We're a long ways from Houston City. O' course, you'll be gettin' off at Hempstead but that's much nearer to Houston City than to here."

Becky leaned back in her seat and picked up the book that Sally had given her. Sally said that it was all the rage among the young women of San Antonio. She said that her circle of friends would meet several times each week to discuss each chapter. She opened the volume and read the title, *Little Women*. She thought, *Now, who would write a whole book about tiny women. It must be some children's fairy tale?*

Becky awoke with a start. The rhythmic rocking of the

train car had stopped. The book lay open on her lap. *I must be more tired than I thought. I wonder why we are stopped.* She looked out of the window and saw that they were at a small village. The man sitting across the aisle from her said, "Ma'am, I see a big ol' look of consternation on your face. This train don't hardly get going good afore she stops at some little ol' town to drop off or pick up mail and maybe a passenger or two. If it ran straight on through, Austin to Houston City would take no more than the better part of five or six hours. But the fact is, we stop at derned near ever' cotton barn or silo we come to. And, of course, we'll stop to take on water ever' thirty miles or so and wood now and again. We'll be lucky to get to Houston City by dark."

Hempstead was hot, humid, and smelled of pine trees. After her ordeal in the arid, brown of west Texas and Mexico, the green of the countryside was almost overwhelming. Becky had not seen such soggy land since she and her family left Mississippi while she was but a child. The streets were like rivers of mud. The coach that took her from the train station to the hotel wallowed in the mire and slogged along almost up to the hubs. The driver was splattered from the waist down with what the horses' hooves threw up. Mosquitoes swarmed in clouds as she walked across the boardwalk to the hotel entrance. A clerk looked her over and asked, "What can I do for you, Miss?"

"It's Mrs.," said Becky. "I need a room for the night. I'm taking the train to Denison in the morning and need a room."

"Yes, Ma'am, just sign the register here. That'll be two dollars. Supper is at seven and it costs an extra twenty five cents."

Becky paid the man and followed him as he carried her bag up to her room on the second floor. The clerk set Becky's bag down after opening the door to her room. He said, "Ma'am, the skeeters ain't as bad up here on the second floor as what you were swattin' when you walked in but they'll always be a few high flyers what make it up here. Use them nets hanging from the bedposts to keep 'em off of you when you tuck in for the night. Anything else I can do for you now?"

"No, that will be all for now. And, thank you for warning me about the mosquitoes."

After the clerk left, Becky removed the clothing from her suitcase and hung the other two dresses that she had bought in San Antonio in the armoire in the corner of the room.

The room was small but well furnished. Besides a bed and the armoire, there was an overstuffed chair in one corner and a small table with a basin and water pitcher across from the bed. A mirror hung on the wall above the table. A poorly drawn portrait of Sam Houston hung in a sad looking frame above the bed.

Becky poured a bit of water into the basin and washed her face. She looked out of the window onto the muddy street for a minute or two before she settled into the chair and thought, *I'm not the simple girl I was a year ago. James is dead and I've wept my tears. Buck is God knows where chasing those Comanches and here I am on my own in this bog of a town. What will I do when I get home? Well, I guess that will have to wait. I'm not going downstairs to wade in all that mud and battle those mosquitoes. I'll just rest up a bit and then go down to see what these folks call supper.*

Supper was not much different from what she often ate back home. The fried catfish was tasty and the biscuits were good. The walls of the dining room were papered with a reddish background on which small blue flowers were printed. Becky thought that the paper was attractive as were the lamps and the other furnishings. The diners were seated on benches at the sides of two long wooden tables. A handsome man seated across from Becky had longish light brown hair and sported a long drooping mustache. As he reached for a biscuit from the platter to his left, his vest swung open to reveal a shiny badge pinned to his shirt. Becky introduced herself and asked, "Are you the town sheriff or a deputy?"

"No, Ma'am," he replied, "I'm Bert Peters, a U.S. Marshal, sent here to take some Army deserters back to Fort Richardson for a Court Marshal and likely a hangin' or a firin' squad. Down yonder at the end of the table, that feller wearin' the Yankee uniform is a sergeant who came to identify the men and help me haul them up to Dallas and then over to the fort at Jacksboro for trial. If the Army don't hang 'em or shoot 'em, I'll haul them over to Corsicana where they robbed the bank. The local Sheriff and town folk would dearly love to get their hands on them. Fact is, that's why I'm along with the Sergeant. I'm to see to it that the Corsicana folks don't try to drag the crooks off the train when we pass through. I hope this conversation don't offend your delicate sensibilities, Ma'am?"

"It would take a lot to offend me by talk after what I have been through," replied Becky. She gave a brief description of her capture by the Comanches and asked, "Will you be traveling on the morning train to Dallas? I'll be on it returning to my parents' home in the Nations."

"Yes, Ma'am, we'll sure enough be on that train. You say your parents live up in the Nations. Is your Paw a preacher or an Indian Agent?"

"No, my father is Choctaw as am I."

"No offense, Ma'am, but I took you for a Creole outta New Orleans not an Injun."

"We Choctaws are civilized and live much the same as you whites. My father is a farmer and my dead husband was a storekeeper. You are sadly misinformed if you think that all Indians are the same."

The train pulled out of Hempstead late in the morning. It clattered in and out of stretches of piney woods as they steamed to the northwest. The morning breeze laced with smoke and ash poured through the open windows of the passenger car in which Becky rode. The breeze brought only small relief from the hot, humid air of an east Texas summer. Occasionally, a farmhouse and barn or fields of corn and cotton drifted by but, mostly, she saw only dense forest. Becky sat near the back of the car on the left-hand side. Other passengers occupied about two-thirds of the seats. Marshal Peters and the Army Sergeant were sitting near the front of the car on the right side. Their two prisoners sat directly in front of them and were shackled to the iron armrests.

The blistering summer sun hung low in the sky as the train pulled into Corsicana. The Army Sergeant stood at the front of the railcar with his revolver drawn. Marshal Peters was likewise positioned at the rear of the car. Becky looked out of the window and expected to see an armed crowd but saw only a few folks disembarking and a few stepping up into the train.

Three men and one woman found seats in the car in which Becky sat. One of the men looked to her like a cowman or rancher. He wore a broad brimmed hat, leather vest, and high-heeled boots that were ornately tooled and reached nearly to his knees. He nodded to Becky and said, " Ma'am." He placed some heavy saddlebags on the window seat across the aisle from Becky and then sat down in the aisle seat. The other two men looked to her to be businessmen of some sort since they wore dark grey suits and bowler hats. The woman was dressed modestly in a print blouse and brown skirt but she wore a large frilly hat and carried a collapsed parasol. She sat directly behind where Marshal Peters and the Sergeant had been sitting. They had left their hats on the seats to show that they were occupied. The men in bowler hats sat behind the woman with the parasol.

As the train lurched out of the station, the Sergeant and the Marshal relaxed and returned to their seats. Becky tired of reading and drifted off to sleep as the train rocked along. She awoke with a start but knew not why.

As Becky looked up, she saw the woman with the

parasol stand up and pull a sawed-off, double-barreled shotgun from the parasol. The woman leveled the shotgun at the back of the Marshal and Sergeant. Meanwhile, the two men in the bowler hats stood up and one of them said, "Marshal, stand up and keep your hands where we can see them. You, too, Army boy. Thelma's got a scattergun aimed at your backs."

After her experience with the attempted robbery of the stage from San Antonio to Austin, Becky had bought a .32 caliber pocket pistol from a store near the Austin hotel. Becky stepped into the aisle and said in a loud voice, "You three drop your guns or I'll blow a hole right through you."

Just as she said that, she heard the sound of metal rubbing leather followed by the loud click of a revolver being cocked. Out of the corner of her eye, she saw the blue steel of a long barrel pointed straight ahead. In a deep voice the cowman said, "Okay, you Jaspers, ya heard the little lady. Drop them guns and kick 'em into the aisle. And, Thelma, Darlin', lay that scattergun down in the aisle real gentle like. I'd hate to shoot a lady on a fine evenin' like this."

Marshal Peters reached over, picked up the shotgun, and then turned to face his three would-be assailants and his two rescuers. "Much obliged, Mizz Becky, and you, too, sir," he said. "Okay, you three, what's your story?"

Thelma said, "The folks in Corsicana put up a five-hundred dollar reward for your two prisoners. My brothers and I thought it would not do the Army any harm if the citizens of Corsicana got to hang them, and why not? We would be doing a civic service and the reward would help us move to San Francisco."

Marshal Peters said, "Well, the folks in Corsicana are goin' to be deprived of the honor and you three will stand trial in Federal Court for obstructing a Federal Officer in the performance of his duties. Sit down and keep your hands on the back of the seats in front of you." He rang for the conductor and when he arrived, Marshal Peters requested that he return with some rope. The Conductor replied that the railroad did not keep a supply of rope aboard.

"Son," said the Cowman to the Conductor, "go look in the baggage car. My braided, horse hair lariat is tied with a piggin' string to my saddle." He turned to Marshal Peters and said, "Marshal, I'm Jim Loving. You've likely heard of my family or at least my Dad. Since his death, I've taken over the family cattle business and moved to my ranch over in Jack County. I favor a Mexican saddle maker in Corsicana and was there to pick up a new saddle and have my old one repaired. I 'spect your prisoners are two of those deserters I heard tell about. You're welcome to borrow my lariat. Just don't cut it. It was my Dad's and I'm sorta sentimental about it. I'll send one of my hands over to the Fort to pick it up when you're done with it."

"No need for that," said Peters, "I'll turn these three over to the Sheriff in Dallas and return your rope then. Since we won't get to Dallas until late tonight, I expect that you'll be staying there before leaving for your ranch."

"That's right, I'll be staying at the hotel across from the railway station. Just get it over to me by nine in the morning." He turned to Becky and said, "Ma'am, I admire your sand. Please allow me to treat you to a late supper when we get to Dallas."

"Thank you, sir, but I'll be staying aboard this train all the way to Denison."

"Well, if you ever make it out to Jack County, have somebody direct you to the ranch. I'd be happy to show you a good time, and I'd like my wife and family to meet you."

It was after two a.m. when the train finally pulled into Denison. Becky stepped out onto the platform and was engulfed in her mother's arms. Papa stood back for a moment before he also embraced her. He said with tears in his eyes, "Becky girl, we thought we had lost you. You can't know how good it is to see you well and strong. We have rooms for us over at the hotel. Let's go and rest. We have a long wagon ride in the morning and we can catch up on all your news then."

Late the next morning after a big breakfast, Becky and her parents loaded their things into the family wagon and set out for the ride home.

VI

After several weeks as part of Major Jones' escort, Buck rotated back to Company F. Major Jones' policy was to keep rotating men on and off of his personal escort so that he could evaluate who to keep and who to cut should the legislature require future reductions in the size of the force. During his last trip to Austin, he had heard rumors that some members of the legislature, especially those from the eastern part of Texas, were reluctant to keep the Frontier Battalion at full strength.

On a muggy, hot September morning, Buck and ten of his men were sent out on a scout following a report of Indians on the Medina River. The Rangers found a small group of bee hunters camped near the river.

Mr. Judson, the leader of the group, stood next to a wagon loaded with honey kegs and said, "I shore am glad to see you Rangers. Injuns slipped on us three nights ago and made off with all of our horses. I see my boy made it to Bandera to send a message fer you boys to come. He'll be along directly with more horses fer us. Let me show you where the tracks lead."

"We did not see your boy or get your message," said Buck. "We happened on your camp by chance. We'll do our best to try to recover your livestock but, as you can see, our mounts are in bad shape. There's hardly any grass left between the head of the Llano all the way down to the Nueces. The Indians have burned it off to keep us Rangers penned up at the head of the Guadalupe. Plus, we're short of grain that we usually carry with us."

San Saba Gold

The Rangers followed the trail as far as the Nueces River before giving up the chase. The terrain between the Medina and the Nueces is a mixture of steep hills cut through with rough, rocky canyons. The combination of the rough terrain, lack of grass, and daily temperatures over one hundred degrees exhausted both men and horses. The Indians were too well mounted and had too much of a head start for the Rangers to overcome.

At the riverbank Buck held up his fist and said, "That's it, boys, we're gonna have to let this bunch go. Let's camp here and rest a day before returning to Company headquarters. We'll be lucky to get back with our own horses. They're plumb played out. There's a little grass here and there along the river. We can picket the horses here and all go out tomorrow afoot scroungin' whatever grass we can cut. Bill, you and Jim, will stand guard over the horses while the rest of us gather feed."

✳✳✳

Four days later, the troop straggled back into the Company camp at the head of the Guadalupe. A tropical storm that had blown out most of its fury but not all of its rain on the northern Mexico coast had drifted across south central Texas. It had rained every day since Buck and his men had started home from the Nueces. Between the heavy rains and the high water they had to cross at the rivers and creeks, the men were soaked and miserable. Buck saw to his horse and then reported to Captain Coldwell's tent to make his report.

"What do you have to report, Sergeant?" asked Captain Coldwell.

Buck read from his written report, "On August twenty-fourth, we found six white bee hunters camped next to a wagon load of honey on the Medina River about twenty miles above Bandera. Durin' the night of the twentieth or twenty-first of August, four Indians stole ten horses from the men while they slept. The bee hunters had no guard posted. From the tracks, it appears that the Indians arrived on foot and took the horses without havin' interest in the men or the honey. We trailed the tracks west across rough country and crossed the

Sabinal River where we camped for the night. From there, the Indians had driven the stolen horses, four of which they rode, of course, west and crossed the Frio River just below Leakey Springs. After crossin' the Frio, the trail cut sharply southwest and hit the Nueces about ten miles south of Camp Wood. That bein' the end of our jurisdiction and given the sorry condition of our horses, I ordered the men to abandon the chase. The Indians were better mounted than us and had plenty of fresh mounts to switch to. We rested our mounts and ourselves for one day on the Nueces and returned here as directly as possible. My guess is that they were either Kickapoos or Lipans coming up out of Old Mexico."

"Very well, Sergeant," said Captain Coldwell. "See to your men and get some food and rest yourself."

"Yes, sir," replied Buck.

In late September of 1874, Colonel Ranald S. Mackenzie and troops of the U.S. 4th Cavalry attacked the Comanche stronghold at Palo Duro Canyon in the Texas Panhandle. During the engagement, the troops routed the Indians, destroyed the tepees and their winter supplies. The 1,400 Comanche ponies were all killed save a few that were awarded to Tonkawa scouts who had guided the troops to the village. Most of the fleeing Comanches moved to the reservations in the Indian Nations. The loss of their winter provisions and horses effectively brought an end to large-scale raids by the southern Plains' Indians. Small bands of warriors did continue to raid for some time. As it happens, neither the Rangers nor the rest of Texans along the frontier were aware of Mackenzie's victory.

After a few days of rest, Buck and five of his men were sent out to the area known as 'The Devil's Backbone' between the towns of Blanco and Wimberley's Mill. Captain Coldwell had received reports of missing cattle from the ranchers along the river in the area. Over the eons, the Blanco River has carved its way through steep sided, cedar-covered limestone hills. The Blanco River, except during periods of heavy rain, runs crystal clear and shallow across a wide, snow-white limestone bottom.

Buck and his men rode up to a log 'dog-run' ranch house a few miles east of the confluence of the Blanco and Little Blanco rivers. As was the custom of the country, they reined up fifty yards out and Buck hailed the house. A thin middle-aged woman stepped out on the gallery along the front of the house. She wore a faded cotton dress and low-heeled leather boots. She held a double-barreled shotgun in her hands.

"Who are you and what do you want?" she asked.

"We're Rangers, Ma'am, and we've come to look into the cattle stealin' in this area," said Buck.

She replied, "Well, y'all come on over and help yourselves to the well. I'll get Pat. He's out back doctorin' a horse with a split hoof. And, yep, we're missin' near to twenty head, almost all we got on this little spread."

Buck dismounted and handed his reins to one of his men. He and the woman walked around to the back of the house where her husband was working. Pat dropped the horse's hoof and stood up. Pat Whittaker was tall and thin with a fringe of brown hair below the brim of his beat up felt hat. He wore faded black pants that had worn white at the knees and seat. His old blue shirt showed hard use as well. Like most hill country ranchers, he had worked himself old before his time. Pat asked, "Who's this feller, Sary?"

Buck introduced himself and said, "Tell me whatever you can about your cattle. When were they taken? Are they branded?"

"Yes, sir, they carry my Circle PW brand on their left hip. They come up missin' about a week ago. I keep 'em over yonder acrost the river in that flat. I got up one mornin' and they was gone. Tracks led west but they was a goodly many more tracks than my twenty would-a made. I rode over to the neighbor's place and he said near ever'body down river for ten miles is missin' stock.   Injuns don't normally mess with beeves, so I reckon it was white or Meskin rustlers."

"Let's go take a look at those tracks," said Buck.

Buck stepped down from his saddle to examine the tracks. It had rained the day before the cattle were stolen, so the tracks were clear in the dried mud. "Looks like maybe eighty head," said Buck, "and at least five shod horses. One of the thieves' horses throws his left hind leg a bit to the side when he steps. Jim, look here in these tracks in the caliche. See how that track kinda skids out to the left ever' time he steps."

Buck took his little tally book out of his shirt pocket and jotted a few notes. He said, "Can you give me the brands your neighbors use? That way we can get the cattle back where they belong if we can catch these skunks."

After Buck made note of the brands, he said, "Thanks, Mr. Whittaker.   We'll see where these tracks lead and maybeso we'll get your cattle back."

The Rangers followed the tracks west until a half-mile before they reached the confluence of the two rivers, the tracks turned south. As they topped a rise and stopped to let their horses blow, Buck spotted buzzards circling low over a little draw a mile or so ahead.

"Oh-oh," said Buck, "lookee yonder, boys.   There's something dead in that draw and these tracks are headin' that way."

As they rode toward where the buzzards circled, the south breeze brought the strong smell of decay.

"Let's swing around and come at it from the upwind side," said Buck, "I don't know about you fellers, but I've had all this perfume I need and my pony ain't real eager to keep smellin' this either."

"Hide thieves!" exclaimed Buck.   "Look at all that wasted beef. Scout around and see if you can find tracks leading away."

"Over here, Buck," said Ranger Baker. "Wagon tracks headin' off to the south."

The Rangers stopped at Fischer's Store to camp for the night. Buck walked into the store, introduced himself, and asked the storekeeper, "You seen a wagon load of green hides come past here about a week ago? We're trackin' a group of hide thieves."

"No, sir, I never did but about that time I heard a wagon and some riders pass through in the middle of the night. If'n they's stolen hides, them boys likely took 'em on to San Antone where the buyers don't ask a lot of questions."

Buck walked back to where the Rangers were building a fire to heat coffee and cook their supper. "Boys, I reckon we come up with an empty sack. The tracks we were followin' are so mixed in with others now that we'll never know for sure where they went. The storekeeper says they likely went to San Antonio. I'll have the Captain write to the town Marshal. The Marshal can check with local tanners and hide buyers to see if anyone bought hides carrying that Circle PW brand or any of the other brands that Whittaker listed for us. In the mornin', we'll head back to camp."

VII

In November, Buck rotated back onto Major Jones' escort while Company F was reassigned to Hildago County to deal with outlaws along the border with Mexico. One day, two of Captain Perry's Company D Rangers raced into camp and reported that they had been attacked by a party of Comanches not more than five miles away. Under the command of Lieutenant Beavert, Buck and Ranger Charley Wood rode out after the Comanches.

"Buck, you and Charley are our best trackers," said the Lieutenant. "Ride on out and see if you can pick up the trail."

"Yes, sir," replied Buck as he and Charley Wood spurred their horses to a gallop.

A little over five miles out from camp, Buck picked up the trail of the Comanches. "Looks like nine of 'em," he said. "I'd say they've got at least an hour on us. Let's git after 'em."

Meanwhile, a detachment from Captain Perry's Company led by Lieutenant Dan Roberts raced to join Lieutenant Beavert. Lieutenant Roberts' party of Rangers had just ridden into camp after Beavert's group left. They had been out on a scout looking for the Comanches based on reported raids in the county. They spurred their mounts to a gallop to catch up with Buck and Charley. Lieutenant Beavert trailed behind.

"It looks like they're followin' the Little Saline Creek," said Buck. "You scoot back and see what's keepin' the Lieutenant. I don't think we're more'n a few minutes behind the Comanches now. They're jist moseyin' along this little creek. Tell Lieutenant Beavert that he'd best come a-runnin'."

Buck headed up the creek as Charley turned back toward the Lieutenant. Twenty minutes later, the tracks left the creek and led west out onto the open prairie. As Buck was topping a little rise, he heard the Lieutenant Roberts and his Rangers closing from behind. Lieutenant Roberts and Corporal Thurlough Weed were in the lead as they came along side Buck.

Buck said, "They're jist over this little rise, less than a half mile ahead of us."

The Rangers rode over the rise and could see the Comanches riding slowly along in single file just ahead. Surprisingly, the Comanches turned to fight rather than attempting to outrun the Rangers. The two sides were nearly equal in numbers though the Rangers had a slight advantage.

Lieutenant Roberts' men were equipped with the Sharps rifles issued to them by the state. The rifles were accurate but slow to reload.

Lieutenant Roberts said, "Okay, boys, let's see if we can ease into pistol range before the shootin' starts. Once we start shootin', aim for their horses. The horses are a bigger target and a Comanche afoot isn't so much of an enemy."

Although it made no good sense to Buck, the Ranger practice was to dismount and stand behind their horses in a battle. They would shoot across their horses' backs using the horse as a shield of sorts. Buck thought, *We'll likely be told to dismount which makes no derned sense fightin' horse Indians but orders is orders.*

At that moment, the Comanches' leader charged straight at the Rangers. His second shot hit Lieutenant Roberts' horse in the shoulder. Roberts jumped from his horse before the animal could fall and pin him. He stood behind his injured horse, took aim with his rifle at the onrushing Comanche, and shot him from his pony. He was dead before he hit the ground.

Another Comanche had flanked Lieutenant Roberts so as to get a clear shot. As he aimed his rifle, Corporal Weed shot him through the heart. The remaining Comanches wheeled their ponies around and fled in several directions. The Rangers remounted and scattered in pursuit.

Lieutenant Roberts plodded along on his wounded mount beside Ranger George Bryant who was riding a pitiful nag. Even though they were moving slowly, they managed to overtake two Comanches riding double on a horse. Bryant killed the Comanche on the back of the horse with a pistol shot. Before he could shoot again, the Comanche horse balked and refused to move. It had been worn down by running with two men on its back. Roberts and Bryant captured the second Comanche who gave up without a struggle. Corporal Weed galloped over to help and was left in charge of the prisoner and his weapons.

Corporal Bryant and Lieutenant Roberts took up the chase again along with their comrades. Two Comanches darted from a thicket right in front of them. Roberts and Bryant killed both of the Comanches during an exchange of fire. Their chasing was over, as Roberts' injured horse could go no further.

The Company D Rangers' horses were exhausted from the chase and the scout they had been making. Roberts called his men back and ordered them back to camp. Lieutenant Beavert, Buck, and Charley galloped on in pursuit of the fleeing Comanches. They drew close enough for a running battle and wounded one of the Comanches without sustaining injury to themselves or their horses. Just before dark, the Comanches rode down into a deep rock overhang along a creek and dismounted. Buck, Charley, and Lieutenant Beavert dismounted and concealed themselves behind some trees. They had the Comanches cornered but were too few in number to attack them.

"Charley," said Lieutenant Beavert, "Buck and I will keep them pinned in. You ride north to Menardville to get some help. It can't be more than twenty-five or thirty miles from our position. It'll be dark soon and I want you back by morning."

Charley rode off in the direction of Menardville as Buck and Beavert fired into the darkness of the cave-like overhang. Twice, they heard a Comanche cry out following their shots but soon it was too dark to see much, so they sat quietly listening for any movement by the Comanches or their horses.

As dawn broke, Buck eased up to the overhang.

"Lieutenant, they're gone. Look's like we killed one of 'em from all the blood over here and wounded another over there. I 'spect we should give up the chase. We licked 'em pretty good."

"Okay, come on back. Let's head toward Menardville and see if we can meet Charley on his way back."

Buck had found the running battle exciting, at least, more so than the usual Ranger tactic of dismounting and firing over the saddles of their horses. His hatred for the Comanches and Kiowas still burned in his chest, even though the scalps of White Elk, Black Hand, and Little Hawk hung from his saddle horn. They had killed his grandfather and older cousin and had stolen Becky. As a boy, he had been unable to avenge his mother's death by renegade soldiers of the Union Army, but as a man he intended to kill as many Comanches and Kiowas as he could within the law.

VIII

In late 1874, Major Jones faced a budgetary crisis. Under the Appropriation Act, the defense funds were to support the Frontier Battalion and any other local militias formed by the legislature or governor. These local militias tended to be short-term to deal with some immediate need but they severely drained the small appropriation. The Major had to choose between keeping the Battalion at full strength for a few months or drastically downsizing and hoping for a future appropriation. He chose the latter.

By early 1875, the force was reduced from 470 men to approximately 200. The Company Captains were given the option of leaving the force or accepting a pay reduction with a decrease in rank to Lieutenant. Each Company commander was told to cut his force to approximately thirty men. Voluntary resignations were requested and, if that was insufficient to reach the target strength, the commanders dismissed whomever they chose.

Buck was torn between his desire to visit Becky and what he felt was his duty to stay with the Rangers. He and Becky had exchanged a few letters since their parting. Her first letter to him was a relief since she informed him that she was safely back home with her parents. He enjoyed her descriptions of her adventurous trip home and was proud that she showed spunk with the desperadoes she had encountered. He had told her of the various Ranger 'scouts' he had been on and of his pride in most of his fellow Rangers.

In Becky's last letter, she had hinted that she would like to see him and have him involved in less dangerous activities.

Major Jones was sitting and writing at his desk in his tent when Buck stuck his head inside. "Major, sorry to interrupt but may I have a word or two?"

"Yes, Sergeant, What is it?"

"Sir, it's about these troop reductions. I'd like to stay on but I've got some personal business that needs attention up in the Nations."

"Buck, I want you as a permanent member of my escort so that I can send you wherever I deem your skills will benefit the Battalion. If you will agree to stay for at least another year, I'll grant you a temporary leave without pay for six weeks. Is that long enough to resolve your family matter?"

"Yes, sir, thank you, sir. I'll be back as soon as I can but no later than six weeks."

"Okay, Buck, come by my tent in the morning. I'll have these reports ready by then and you can take them to the Adjutant General in Austin for me. Your leave can commence once the delivery is made."

As Buck walked away from the Major's tent, he chuckled to himself, *Leave without pay! Hell, we rarely get paid for active duty. No great loss.*

After Buck had made his delivery to the Adjutant General in Austin, he sold his bay pony and bought a pack mule.

He purchased supplies for his trip and loaded the mule. He intended to ride Patch. He set out north on the old Chisholm Trail laid out years earlier by the trader Jesse Chisholm. He camped near the big 'Round Rock' where the trail crossed Brushy Creek just west of the little town named for the rock. The big paint horse could eat up the miles but Buck wanted to take his time. He figured to branch onto the Shawnee Trail at Waco and follow it most of the way to the

Nations. He would need a good three days to reach Waco and another four to reach his Grandfather's store in the Nations. If the weather held, it should be an easy trip and restful being away from Ranger duties for a change.

It was late February and the nights were chilly in Central Texas so Buck rolled up in a buffalo robe he had bought from a trader in Austin. He knew it would get colder the further north he traveled. The robe was heavy and costly but it would be worth every penny if a Blue Norther blew in. As he looked up at the sky filled with stars, he thought, *I wonder what I ought to do about Becky? After this year is up with the Rangers, I may not be ready to take up life as a storekeeper again. I can't expect her to wait around on me forever. And, who's to say that she don't already have another feller picked out. Since I'm not full blood Choctaw, her parents were against me courtin' her back afore she fell in love with James. I wonder if they have changed their minds on that? Oh well, no since frettin' about that now, what'll be will be.*

Buck was a day and a half north of Dallas and almost to his destination when a Blue Norther hit. The temperature dropped forty degrees in less than an hour. The howling wind drove blinding sleet into his face and the faces of his animals. The mule, having more sense than the man or the horse in such matters, balked and refused to move north. Instead, he turned his back to the wind and brayed in protest. "Well, sir, that's all she wrote fer today," said Buck aloud.

He eased back south and found a little gully for them to duck into. Fortunately, the gully was wide enough and deep enough to get them out of the wind plus it had a little stream of water running through it. He hobbled the horse and mule, grained them, and built himself a bit of a tent using the buffalo robe and some brush. "It ain't much but it's home," laughed Buck. He got a little fire going under an overhang in the gully wall and wrapped strips of bacon on sticks that he angled over the fire. *I've eaten a lot worse and a lot less,* he thought.

The sleet turned to snow around midnight but the cold front had passed through by dawn. Although it was cold, the sky was as blue as it gets and the wind was down to a light breeze. Buck packed the mule, saddled Patch, and mounted for the last day of the trip. The horse and the mule were frisky in the cool air so Buck let them run for a few miles before settling back to a lope.

At the crossing, the Red River is a quarter mile wide expanse of red sand with a fifty-yard wide, foot or two deep ribbon of tomato-colored water snaking through the sand. The trick with the type of quicksand in the Red River is to keep moving. You stop and you sink. So Buck touched his spurs to the horse's flank and gave the mule's lead rope a tug. They splashed across without incident. "Just a couple or three hours to the store, then you boys can rest," he said to his stock. The horse nickered as though he understood and the mule brayed twice in agreement.

★★★

Buck placed his saddle on the rack in his grandfather's barn and hooked the rest of his tack and gear on big nails sticking out from the barn's support posts. He turned the horse and mule out into the five-acre horse trap behind the barn and walked up to the house. He knocked on the door and when no one answered, he opened the door and stepped in. No one was home. He found some leftover biscuits in the kitchen and sliced a slab of meat from a ham hanging from a hook in the pantry. *I reckon Luke's over to the store,* he thought.

Buck walked over to the store, stepped up onto the gallery, and stuck his head in the door. "Anybody here?" he asked.

Before Luke could close his gaping mouth to answer,

Buck rushed over to him and gave him a bear hug. "Laws, but it good to see you, Luke. I see you made it back from the Comancheria in one piece and looks like you're prosperin' as a storekeep."

Luke stammered, "B-B-Buck, where'd you come from?"

"I'm on temporary leave from the Texas Rangers and came home for a visit. Tell me all the news from around here."

Luke replied, "I was just fixin' to close for the noon hour. Let's go over to the house and get some lunch. We can catch up on each other's news over there. I'll put a sign on the door here so if anybody comes to buy anything from the store, they can walk over to the house and fetch me."

After they had finished their stories, Buck asked, "Have you seen Becky? How is she and does she seem okay?"

Luke grinned like a mule eating briars through a wire fence. "Still kinda sweet on her, huh? Yes, I see her now and again when she and her Maw come to the store. She never says much to me about her time with the Comanches but I figure it's none of my business anyhow. She does seem happy enough so I guess she wasn't treated too badly. Oh, there's a big dance over to the meeting hall tonight. I bet a Yankee dollar she'll be there."

"Well, let's go to the dance. I'll surprise her. Next week, I want you to go with me over to Durant Station and see Granddad's lawyer. I want to sign the store over to you and make out a will in case I don't get back from Texas next time."

"Well, Buck, you oughta keep a share in the store. By rights, it's half yours. I don't have enough ready cash to buy out your half."

"No, sir, you've been keepin' it goin' while I was away and I don't think I'm cut out to be a storekeeper anymore. I'll make you a deal. I'll swap my half interest for a new set of clothes, whatever you got in stock. I'd rather not go to the dance in my Ranger duds. They've gotten a bit trail worn. Plus, I do alright on my Ranger pay." Buck knew that was a lie since the Rangers were promised pay but it rarely was actually given.

San Saba Gold

After supper, Luke hitched the team to his springboard and set out to pick up his girl friend, Sarah. Buck caught Patch, saddled him, and headed for the meeting hall. The dance was well underway by the time that Buck arrived. The hall was brightly lit with lanterns. A fiddler was sawing out a lively tune and the dancers were pounding a rhythmic shuffling beat on the wood floor. Buck tied his horse to one of the picket lines that had been stretched between the oak trees that surrounded the meeting hall. He stood for a few minutes outside the glow of the lantern light and looked through one of the windows to see if he could spot Becky.

At first he did not recognize her but what he saw staggered him. She was no longer the Indian girl he knew or the bedraggled girl he had rescued down in Old Mexico. She was a beautiful young woman wearing a long colorful cotton dress, as was the fashion among Choctaw women. Becky sat on one of the benches that lined the walls of the hall. She was talking and laughing with two other young women.

Buck walked to the front of the building and eased through the door. The fiddler had started up a new tune and Buck walked over to where Becky and her friends were sitting. He interrupted, "Excuse me, Ma'am, may I have the honor of this dance?"

Becky looked up to see who was asking and blurted, "No, thank y... uh, uh. Buck, Buck!! What? Where? How did you get here?"

"On horseback, of course," teased Buck. "It is so good to see you. And, I don't really know how to dance very good but I didn't know what else to say."

Becky turned to her friends and said, "Y'all remember Buck from the store over on the Washita, don't you? He's the one that I told you about who rescued me from the Mexicans."

The two young women reintroduced themselves to Buck and then left to get glasses of punch. Buck sat down next to Becky and said, "I've got some business to take care of over in Durant Station on Monday but I'd like to come over to your folks' house on Tuesday to see your folks and visit a bit, if that's okay with you?"

"Don't be silly. Of course, it's okay. My folks will be real glad to see you again. I will look forward to your visit. In the meantime, tell me all about your work with the Rangers. Your letters don't tell me much about what you are doing. In fact, they're a bit short, kind of 'I'm fine and I hope you are too, goodbye'. A girl doesn't get much news out of that."

"I admit that I'm no great shakes of a letter writer. Plus, I didn't figger that you'd be all that interested in scouts for hostile Indians, catchin' outlaws, and the like. Life in the Ranger camp is mostly borin' stuff. We spend most of our time just sitting around or playing games. Every now and again I go hunting for meat for the camp but that's not too often lately."

Just then, Luke and Sarah came into the hall and walked over to where Buck and Becky were sitting. Around the same time, Becky's two friends, Betty and Mildred, returned from the punch bowl. The rest of the evening was spent in dancing, chatting, and laughing at Luke's jokes.

As they left the hall, Becky said, "Goodnight, Buck, I've got to go. My father is waiting there in the wagon."

"I'll be by on Tuesday morning. We can have a long chat then. Goodnight, Becky."

Becky's father was sitting in a rocking chair on the front porch when Buck rode up to the house and dismounted. "Good mornin' Mister Griffin, I'm Caleb McDougal. Do you remember me?"

"Buck, of course, I know you but I'm not used to seeing you so dressed up. Come on up here and get out of the sun. It's turned warm after that norther blew through last week. Becky said that you'd be by this morning."

"Yes, sir, I wanted to come by and pay my respects and maybe talk to you about Becky."

"Believe it or not, I was a young man once and I

suspect you'd like to court Becky like you did before she and James started going together."

"Well, you kinda cut to the chase, don't you? I thought maybe if you'd approve I would like to see if Becky had any interest in seeing me."

"Son, let an old man give you a bit of advice. As you well know, Becky lost her husband less than a year ago. It is only proper for her to respect his memory and not start seeing other fellows for a year or two. She has to put her ordeal and her loss behind her. If she takes up with a new man too soon, James will surely come between them. I am less fixed on the idea of only a pure Choctaw for her than I was a few years ago. You have proved to be a fine and honorable young man but my advice is that you go slow. Time heals most wounds. Give her a little room for now."

"Yes, sir, that's exactly what I've got in mind. You see, I'm only here on a temporary leave from the Texas Rangers. I gave them my word that I'd serve out my enlistment, which could stretch for another year. I wanted to see you and Becky to let her know that I still have feelings for her and see if she would wait for me."

Just then the front door scraped open and Mrs. Griffin stepped out followed by Becky. Mrs. Griffin said, "Why, hello, Buck. I'm so glad to see you and have the opportunity to thank you for rescuing our Becky."

Buck blushed a bit and replied, "It's good to see you again, Ma'am, and there weren't no way I'd have left Becky down yonder."

Mrs. Griffin said, "Buck, Becky has told me what you did to get her back and, since you are here in one piece, I expect that you caught those who took her, or else you could not find them."

"I found 'em all right. They're roastin' in the Devil's campfire these days."

"Momma, the tea's getting cold, let go into the parlor," said Becky.

After an hour or so of chatting, Mrs. Griffin said, "It's a

beautiful day. Why don't you young folks take a little walk while I get us some lunch ready?"

Buck led Becky out of the front door. They walked down to the little creek that ran just beyond the barn and took a seat on a bench that Mr. Griffin had built and placed under a big live oak tree. The creek gurgled across reddish brown rocks. A cardinal sang from a bush somewhere on the other side of the creek, or maybe it was a mocking bird imitating a cardinal, Buck wasn't sure. He turned to Becky and said, "I've only got a couple of weeks before I have to return to my Ranger duties. I want you to know that I respect your need for time to deal with the loss of James. He was my cousin and I loved him like a brother, so I'm hurtin', too. But after a spell, maybe a year or so, I'd like to see if you have any feelin's for me. If you do, I will be asking you an important question."

"Thanks, Buck, for not rushing things. My head is still filled with a jumble of images and my heart is confused and hurt. Let's keep in touch and see how things go." She gave him a punch on the arm and continued, "And, from now on write me letters that tell me more about what you are doing. They won't be boring to me."

San Saba Gold

IX

The weeks flew by. After saying his goodbyes, Buck set out on his return trip to Austin. He had to check in at the Adjutant General's Office to be reinstated to active duty and to see where he was to be assigned. The nights were still cool and the days were glorious. The countryside was awash with wildflowers, especially what were being called Texas Bluebonnets. Buck took his time so as to be easy on his horse and mule but also just to enjoy the ride. For the most part, he avoided the little towns along the way. Occasionally, he would stop in and partake of the hospitality of a farm family. The woods teemed with deer and turkeys and the streams were full of fish. Buck never showed up at a farmhouse door without an ample gift of wild game or fish.

The last night on the trail, Buck camped on Walnut Creek. He was only a few miles from the Capitol but he did not want to pay for a hotel bill or livery fee in town. He could easily arrive at Adjutant General Steele's office when it opened in the morning.

After buying a dark bay gelding at the livery, he went to see General Steele. As he sat in the waiting room, the door to the General's Office opened and Major Jones stepped out. Buck stood up holding his floppy felt hat in his hand. "I'm back and reporting for duty, sir," said Buck.

Major Jones was deep in thought and took a moment to recognize Buck. "Glad to have you back, Sergeant. Walk with me, please."

After they had left the building, Major Jones said, "Buck, General Steele wants for us to concentrate on cattle thievery, murderers, and other outlaws that are overrunning the country from the Nueces to the San Saba. I've got a special job for you. Start here in Travis County and work south to Uvalde. Then work your way back and forth north to Fort Richardson. I want you to make me a book of every recorded brand in each county and any unrecorded brands you come across. Once we have that, we can get copies to each Ranger Company and start cleaning up this cattle stealing and brand burning business. I'll have General Steele's Secretary give you a letter issuing you statewide authority to do this. Also, I'll have a letter of credit drawn up so you can charge supplies to our account, as you need them. I trust you not to abuse it. As you know, the Ranger appropriation is lean. I will see that you get one of our mules for you supplies."

"I have a mule of my own, sir, and I won't charge more supplies than bare essentials."

"Good man, meet me at the General's Office tomorrow morning at nine and I'll have your letters ready. See you then."

"Good day, sir. See you at nine."

After they shook hands and parted, Buck walked over to the County Clerk's Office to get a list of registered brands, if any.

✳✳✳

The Colorado River runs more or less west to east through Travis County, where Austin is located. The river splits the county into roughly equal north and south parts. Similarly, the Balcones Escarpment splits the county into east and west halves. East of the escarpment, the land is comprised of rolling, gentle hills. The dark loam is readily adapted to farming and stock rearing. The western half of the county consists of a series of limestone hills and canyons covered in cedars and other drought-hardy plants. It is too rocky for farming except in a few spots but fine for livestock as long as not too many are placed on the semi-arid land. Goats do well and small cattle outfits can succeed.

After listing the few recorded brands at the County Clerk's Office, Buck walked down to the wagon yard where he had left his animals. He decided to start on the eastern half of the county first since the County Clerk had said that he thought that few of the ranchers in the western half of the county branded their cattle. *I'll just mosey around and see if there are any cattle ranchers and what brands I can find,* thought Buck.

After months and hundreds of miles of riding back and forth through the Texas Hill Country, Buck decided that he had done about as much as he could in compiling a brand book for the Major. Buck sat by his small campfire and looked up the steep side of Packsaddle Mountain right in front of him. *So this is where those ranchers fought the Apaches two or three years ago. And, a feller at the store back in Llano said that Jim Bowie's lost mine was up there somewhere just waiting for somebody to dig out all that silver. Well, sir, it won't be me. I've had folks in San Saba and in Menardville tell me the mine was in a half dozen places over there, too. Just a whole bunch of nonsense, if you ask me. I expect that if Ol' Jim Bowie had a sliver mine, he'd never have been trapped at the Alamo and got himself slaughtered.*

He eased the coffee pot away from the crackling cedar wood fire. He poured a cup and leaned back against his saddle. The horses and mule were hobbled and rustling up whatever they could find to eat. As he did each night, he had Patch tied on the end of a long lead with the other end tied to his saddle horn. The bay was picketed close by. He didn't want the horses to wander too far. In this country, he might need to mount quickly and there was always the threat of horse theft.

Suddenly, he sat up and grabbed his rifle. Something was out there he felt more than heard or saw. Patch gave a nicker followed by a bray from the mule and a snort from the bay. He eased into the darkness away from the fire and crouched behind one of the huge boulders that had tumbled down the mountainside.

"Buck, is that you? Don't shoot, I'm coming in," said a familiar voice.

"Angry, is that you?" Angry, a Lipan Apache, had ridden with Buck on the trail of the Comanches who had killed

Buck's kin and stolen Becky. Angry Who Runs Far was a former Ranger scout who had teamed up with Buck when his own wife and son were killed by the same group of Comanches.

"Buck, I delivered a message to the Sheriff in Llano this morning and he told me that I had just missed seeing you by a few hours. You don't seem to be in a big hurry. It's only fifteen miles or so back to town."

"Nope, I'm on my way back to Austin to deliver a report and feel like I've wasted a sight of time riding around looking at brands on the hind end of cattle. I dread that I'll be given another long list of counties to cover. How about a cup of coffee? And, I can heat up these *frijoles* if you are hungry."

Angry sat on a flat rock near the fire and ate while Buck checked their horses. As Buck returned to the fire, a dog poked his head up from behind Angry. Buck said, "Why hello, Arrow. Remember me, boy?" The dog gave a whine and wagged his tail.

"Angry, how've you been, pardner? What have you been up to and where are you headed?"

"Fine, this and that, and south," replied Angry.

"Great, here I am after wandering to hell and gone for months with nobody to talk to but myself, the horses and that blamed mule. I haven't seen you since you were wounded and all you got to say is three or four words!"

"Good beans," said Angry with a grin.

"Is that it?"

Angry laughed and said, "Okay, here's the short version. That cowman, Patterson, dropped Arrow and me off in Uvalde like he promised. Those folks in Uvalde were none too friendly toward me. It seems they had had a lot of trouble from other Lipans and Kickapoos. So, I took my pony and headed west toward Cal's place out in San Felipe del Rio. I had to go slow because I was still weak and did not want the knife wound to open up again. Cal and Maria took me in and let me recover. Then, the dog and I struck out north. I wanted to go back to my farm on the Concho to place markers on the graves of Yellow Bird and my boys. After carving and placing the stones, I cut south to the Llano River and followed it to town. Along the way, I happened across three Rangers on a scout for some stolen cattle. I knew one of them from the old days when I scouted for the Rangers. He wrote out a message and asked me to deliver it to the Llano town Sheriff who told me where you had headed. And, here I am."

———

"What now, pardner?" asked Buck.

"Texas has bad memories for me. There is too much bad blood between the whites and the Indians. Most of my tribe has been forced out of Texas and now live in Old Mexico or on a reservation over in New Mexico. I plan to join the group down in Old Mexico and resume my life as a farmer. I'll ride along with you as far as Sandy Creek, which will get us past this tall ridge to the west. It's not very far from here, maybe five or six miles. Then, I'll split off to the southwest to avoid San Antonio and go on down to Mexico."

At Sandy Creek, they shook hands and promised to meet again one day. Buck gave Angry some money to help him in his trip to Mexico.

Angry said, "Thank you, Buck, you are a dear friend, and I have something for you."

He handed Buck a leather pouch and said, "There are a dozen or more steel trade points in the pouch. Someday you may decide to make a bow and you will need points for your arrows. You once told me that your mother taught you to make such weapons. *Adios, Amigo.*"

San Saba Gold

X

Lieutenant Coldwell said, "Buck, I want you to take four or five of your men out on a scout up toward the head of the Llano River where the James River dumps into the Llano. See if you can pick up any Indian sign. We got a report of twenty head of missing stock and a dead cowhand from a rancher named Schultz who runs a little spread on the James River between Mountain Home and Mason. The message I got says it was Comanches. I doubt it since it was supposed to have happened in the dark of the moon. Every derned fool in this part of Texas knows the Comanches and Kiowas almost always raid around or on the full moon. Anyhow, I'd start at Schultz's place and see where that leads you."

"We'll head out a first light," said Buck.

Buck and four of his men rode up over the steep hills north of Kerrville and up the valley formed by Johnson Creek to the little settlement of Mountain Home. They bought a slab of bacon from one of the farmers and cooked a hasty meal of biscuits and bacon. Nearly everyone they met spoke German to one another.

Jim Baker, one of Buck's Rangers, explained, "The Germans settled this area of Texas back in the forties on a land grant given to the King of Prussia or some such grandee. Most of 'em are up around Fredericksburg but they are startin' to scatter out along the rivers. I bet a cold beer this feller, Schultz, don't speak much English. He sounds like a Dutchman to me."

"Well, he wrote a letter in English to Lieutenant Coldwell that got us this assignment, so I 'spect we can understand him good enough," said Buck. "'Sides, I don't think he'll be of much help other than to show us where the cowhand was killed and where his stock was pastured."

The next morning, they rode up to the Schultz spread about an hour before noon. Herr Schultz was a big red-faced man with hands like bear paws. His stone cabin was tucked against a hillside facing the James River. He had built a big barn, far nicer than his cabin, and a series of stock pens. He stood in front of the cabin with his arms folded across his bare chest as the Rangers rode up.

"About time choo Rangers showed up," said Herr Schultz. "Ve got no protection out here. De Sheriff in Fredericksburg says ve not in his county. Vhat choo going to do about my cattle and my José vhat vas kilt?"

Buck swung down from his saddle. Buck towered over the short barrel of a man that Schultz was. "Now don't git feisty with us," said Buck. "We're here to try and git your cows back and catch whoever kilt your Mexican. Show us where all this killin' and stealin' took place."

Karl Schultz saddled a dun mare and led the Rangers north along the river for two miles before pointing to a pasture lined with a low limestone wall. He then said, "Here's vhere my cattle vas grazing vhen dem thieves took 'em. I fount poor José over der full of arrows and butchered like a hog. He vas cut from one end to the odder mit his innerds strung across the field. I never see such a t'ing."

Buck said to his men, "You boys dismount and start circling around lookin' fer tracks. It's been a week but there ain't been no rain so we should cut their trail, probably north along the river. A couple of you check from the other side of the river, in case they crossed. I 'spect we're huntin' Comanches or Kiowas from what Herr Schultz has told us."

He turned to Herr Schultz and said, " 'Less you got anything else to add, we'll take it from here. We'll git your cattle back if we can find 'em. I'll git word to you either way. Thanks fer your help. Oh, do you have the arrows that kilt your man? They might help us know who we're after."

"No, I burnt dem vit José's bloody clothes. Chust git de murderin' savages and my cattle." Herr Schultz turned his horse back to the east and rode off cursing to himself in German.

Buck joined the two men searching along the west bank of the river. After thirty minutes of fruitless searching, two pistol shots rang out from east of the river. Buck mounted and splashed through the shallow swift-running water. Bill Sanders was waving his hat over his head on a little saddleback between two hills to the northeast. Buck and the other Rangers trotted over to where Bill waited. Buck dismounted and walked over to where Bill was pointing.

"Good eye," said Buck. "Looks like four unshod ponies pushing the cattle off this way. Wind's blowed out the tracks down below, but that little seep comin' out of that hillside left this spot muddy enough fer the tracks to stay. Let's spread out in a line and see if we can pick up the tracks again headin' west. It looks like they were followin' this game trail, but they may try to trick us by veerin' off, so keep your eyes peeled sharp."

They picked up the tracks off and on for the next twenty miles as they headed almost due north. If Comanches or Kiowas were involved, it would be more likely that they would be heading west. Buck rode out ahead to take a look from a tall hill off to the northwest. From the hilltop, he spotted a spiral of buzzards on the northern horizon. He galloped down to his men and said, "Looks like they slaughtered one or more of the cattle up ahead. There's buzzards circlin'. Let's see if we can git there before dark."

They rode off at a gallop and slowed as they approached the rotting carcasses of the twenty cattle. "Look's like hide thieves," said Buck. "I never heard o' no Comanche hide thieves. It's dern near to dark. Let's move off upwind and camp fer the night. We'll see what we can find in the way o' tracks come mornin'."

All night the Rangers could hear the snarls and yips as coyotes and wolves fought over the dead cattle. At one point, Buck rose up from his blanket on one elbow and said, "You'd think with all that meat layin' out there, the derned varmints could gorge themselves without bickering all night and keeping me awake."

After breaking camp the next morning, the Rangers rode in a wide circle around the dead livestock. They found wagon tracks leading off in the direction of Mason. Buck sent Bill Sanders back to report to Herr Schultz that his cattle had been all killed by hide thieves, not Indians. He sent the other three Rangers back to Kerrville along with a report to Lieutenant Coldwell. He set out at a lope toward Mason.

Now why would a group of hide thieves try to disguise their attack as though they were Comanches? thought Buck. *Seems like a lot o' extra trouble to cover their crime. O' course, maybe they figured that the German would decide it was Comanches and too risky to chase 'em. Who knows?*

Buck inquired about hide buyers at the General Store in Mason. He was directed to a hide trader named Hooper at the west end of town. He dismounted in front of the little tannery. Buck walked around to the back of the building and found three men working hides through a big vat of lime and water to loosen the hair. The oldest of the three turned to Buck and said, "Howdy, *compadre*, what can I do fer you?"

"I'm a Sergeant in the Texas Rangers and my men and I are on the trail of some cattle thieves. Have you bought any hides in the last week or so with a Lazy S brand on them?"

"Yes, sir, I bought twenty green hides a week ago from a group of cowmen who said they had been drivin' twenty head up from the Frio River country when the cattle got into some bad water and started dyin' on 'em. They said that they didn't want a total loss so they skinned 'em out. I give 'em forty dollars fer the hides. Why?"

"The cattle were stolen in Kimble County and a cowhand was kilt," said Buck. "Where did these men go after you bought the hides and what did they look like?"

"They headed back home to the Frio country, I guess. They looked like your typical cowmen. I really didn't pay much mind. Their story sounded legit and there ain't no Lazy S registered in Mason County so, as I say, I didn't pay no never mind."

"Did you have them sign your hide book?"

"You bet, come on up front to the office."

The third entry from the bottom of the page showed: '20 hides, good condition, Lazy S brand, Frio County'. In the signature blank was a big letter X.

"Well, that's a big help," said Buck. "The cattle belonged to a man named Schultz running a spread just over the Kimble County line on the James River. I 'spect you'll be hearin' from him about some sort of restitution fer the hides."

"Hell," said Hooper, "I didn't steal his damn cattle. He best leave it be."

"If I hear that your differences weren't settled peaceably, I'll be back," said Buck. "Good day."

Buck walked down the dusty street and into a little saloon. After a quick drink and a plate of beef and beans, he said to himself, *Might as well head fer home, this trail's gone cold.*

★★★

Buck made his report to Lieutenant Coldwell. They both puzzled over why the hide thieves had tried to make the attack appear to be Comanche work. Lieutenant Coldwell said, "I'll send a couple of the boys down to check along the Frio to see if anybody has lost any stock to hide thieves. My guess is the ones who did it are nowhere near the Frio and never were. One thing for sure, anybody mean enough to murder a man over twenty beeves will commit another crime. We'll catch them eventually. Major Jones has a plan for cleaning up this country as soon as the battalion is fully organized."

"How about we send Bill Sanders and Jim Baker? They

were with me on the scout and know the details of the murder and rustling."

"Sounds good.   Have them provisioned with a pack mule and on their way tomorrow."

PART II
1876

San Saba Gold

XI

In 1845, the federal government established a military post in San Antonio. The following year, with the onset of war with Mexico, the Army established a quartermaster depot and training camp in the city. City officials actively lobbied the federal government to establish this as a permanent U.S. military installation. By 1849, San Antonio was named as the headquarters of the U.S. Army Eighth Military District. A number of buildings were rented and the Alamo was leased from the Catholic Church to serve as a storage depot. The local government made several offers of free land to establish a permanent base but the federal government refused the offers.

The Army presence continued but only as a temporary base with sporadic attempts by city groups to make the base permanent. In 1870, a formal proposal was made to Washington but it met with considerable political opposition. Nevertheless by 1875, the Congress had appropriated funds to create a permanent base. However, Secretary of War Belknap illegally refused to release the funds. He resigned in 1876 rather than face charges of impeachment and the funds were released.

Jack Hartright said, "Jeb, we can make this the biggest bank in San Antonio if we can secure a deal to manage the government funds to build the new Army post. I have convinced the Mayor and a majority of the Council to donate those ninety-three acres over at Government Hill to the Army. The Army liaison that I met assured me that the Army will accept the land and begin construction as soon as the funds arrive.

"Jack, you know that every other bank in Texas will be hot to manage those funds. We're going to have some stiff competition."

"I know it but I'm hoping that we have a edge since we know about it now. I'm going to Washington City to get our foot in the door ahead of the crowd."

George Dawson was only a year beyond graduation from West Point and had already been promoted to First Lieutenant for his work in solving a series of thefts of army equipment. He had been given a few weeks leave prior to his reassignment to Fort Russell in the Wyoming Territory. During the leave, he married his childhood sweetheart, Jenny Bascomb, and left her with her parents in East St. Louis. At his new post in Cheyenne, he was summoned to Colonel Morris' office for orders.

"Have a seat, Lieutenant. Washington has ordered us to take on a rather delicate but very important assignment. Those folks down in San Antonio, Texas have pressured Congress to get a new permanent post built there. I received orders to provide escort for the transfer of government funds to pay for the construction. My orders were to obtain one hundred fifty thousand dollars in twenty dollar, gold Double Eagle coins from the mint down in Denver and haul it to Texas. Typical of those desk soldiers in Washington City, they failed to note that the Denver mint does not produce Double Eagles or any gold coins. The damned coins are made over in Carson City, Nevada, but those easterners have no concept of the distances we deal with out here or the size of the mountains we have. Be that as it may, orders are orders. Your record at the Point and in that criminal business in Georgia is exemplary. I will have orders cut for you to go to Nevada to accompany the gold back to Denver. Then, we'll decide the best way to get it down to south Texas. Any questions?"

"Yes, sir. I'm new to this country and scarcely know where Nevada is much less Carson City. I imagine that that much money in gold coins is going to be a bit bulky."

The Colonel laughed, "Yes, I'd say a bit bulky and heavy – 7,500 coins that will weigh more than five hundred pounds. There's a detachment from California that camps out at old Fort Churchill to keep watch in the Carson City area. With all of the gold and silver mining over there and the mint in Carson City, a military presence in the region seemed prudent. They'll help you get the coins up to the Central Pacific rail line in Reno. That will take you to Cheyenne where you can switch to the Denver Pacific. Take it and the gold to Denver where I will meet you. I'll have a detachment meet you here in Cheyenne for the final leg. I've been ordered to take a troop of cavalry to Denver to protect the Mint there. There have been rumors of a group who plan to attack and rob it."

"Yes, sir. When should I leave and I assume this is all to be kept secret?"

"Yes, son, we don't want any word of this to slip out. Check with me day after tomorrow and be ready to travel. Dismissed."

At the desk in the Officers' tent, Lieutenant Dawson wrote a letter to Jenny as he did almost every day. He closed the letter by telling her that he would be out of touch for a few weeks as he was being sent on a special mission further west. *I don't think that violated any secrecy and it will keep Jenny from fretting with the lapse in daily letters,* he thought as he sealed the envelope.

Then he busied himself with packing his small valise. There wasn't much to pack as he only had the uniform that he was wearing, some extra underwear, and a few toiletry items. He left his dress uniform hanging on the rack. There would be no use for that. He sat on his bunk and started to remove his boots when he heard footsteps approach the front of the tent.

"Enter," he said, without waiting for a summons or a request to enter.

A burly Sergeant stepped through the tent flap and said, "Sir, here's a message from the Colonel. He said you'd best read it right away and I have your mount saddled just outside."

"Thank you, Sergeant, I'll get right to it. Give me a minute or two to read it and get my boots back on."

He opened the envelope and quickly read the note inside. The Colonel included scrip for him to use to buy a set of 'plain' civilian clothes at the store in town. The Colonel explained that it might be wise for him to travel out of uniform."

George rode back to camp with a brown paper parcel tied behind the cantle of his saddle. Back in his tent, he changed out of his uniform and into his 'mining engineer' clothes. He had bought a blue heavy cotton shirt, a pair of brown durable trousers, and a 'Boss of the Plains' Stetson hat. He had decided that his boots fit with the civilian clothing and did not need replacement. Thusly donned, he strode over to Colonel Morris' office to return the unspent funds.

"Well, look at you," said the Colonel, "I believe that rig will do just fine. Going for the engineer look, I see."

"Yes, sir, I thought I'd pose as a mining engineer and, if necessary, explain that I'd come out from the east to see the country and hire on to a mining operation. My Illinois accent would give me away as not a born to the west type."

"I can see that I picked the right man for this job. Here are your orders and a requisition for funds to cover your expenses. The bank will honor the requisition, and your rail tickets will be waiting at the depot. Wire me if you have trouble; otherwise, I'll see you in a few weeks. Dismissed."

XII

George, although utterly exhausted, was fascinated by the scenery along the route of the train trip to Reno. Long days and nights of sitting on the hard wooden seats were brutal, even with an occasional walk up and down the aisle. Of course, the train stopped at every little flea-bitten dusty town to pick up or drop off a passenger or two and/or freight. Also, there were frequent delays to take on water and wood or coal. He spent a night at a hotel in Ogden, Utah to rest a bit. He would change trains there anyway as that was where the Union Pacific and Central Pacific lines met.

At Reno, George took another hotel room and a full day of rest before taking the Virginia & Truckee train down to Carson City. At Carson City, he took the room at the St. Charles hotel that had been arranged by Colonel Morris. The registration clerk handed him an envelope and said that a solider had left it a few days back.

Once he had settled into his room, he opened the envelope and read brief letter from a Captain Hamilton. George was instructed to send a message informing Captain Hamilton of his arrival. George could send his message via one of the soldiers stationed at the U.S. Mint.

The next morning, George dressed in his uniform and went downstairs to breakfast. As he was finishing his coffee, a private came in, walked over to his table, saluted, and said, "Sir, I am Private Bishop. I have orders to escort you to a meeting with Captain Hamilton just south of town. I have a mount for you outside."

"Thank you, Private Bishop, let me get a few things from

my room and I'll be right out, say five minutes."

George rode along side Private Bishop and said, "Man, it's good to be in the saddle after days of sitting on hard wooden railcar seats."

"Then, you came from far off?" asked the Private. "In from San Francisco?"

"Nope, I came over the mountains from Wyoming Territory. Where exactly are we going?"

"Captain Hamilton moved our camp a few weeks back to put us closer to town. There has been a spot of trouble between some of the miners and the town merchants over prices for tools and supplies. We had a killin' and had to hang a couple of outlaws that were stirrin' up the feud. The camp is just around the shoulder of that hill in a grove of trees along Clear Creek."

George presented his orders to Captain Hamilton and said, "Sir, should I remain here in your camp or proceed directly back to Carson City and the Mint? I have had a bit over a week to think about this mission and have a few ideas for how we might prepare the funds for shipment."

"What have you got in mind, Lieutenant?"

"Well, sir, I estimate that the total weight of the coins will be a bit over five hundred pounds. That seems a little too much to disguise easily. So, I thought that we could divide the coins into four parcels of about one hundred twenty five pounds each. We could conceal them in the false bottoms of wooden crates filled with mining tools and labeled as such with a destination of Denver. That way, freight handlers would expect for the crates to be heavy and treat them accordingly. I have civilian clothes with me and could have the crates made up in town for my fictitious mining business back in Denver. My West Point training was as an engineer. I can also buy a little lumber and a few hand tools to make the false bottoms in the crates myself so that only you and I will know about them."

"Young man, you seem to have this all worked out. I'll issue you a wagon. Can you manage a team and wagon?"

"Yes, sir, that's no problem and I have sufficient funds from Colonel Morris to pay for the crates and such."

"Well, get your clothes changed while I have a wagon and team brought up. I suggest that you take a room in town rather than arouse suspicion by driving back and forth to our camp. There is an adequate boarding house run by a Mrs. Tolbert near Doc Benton's livery. Take a room there. Since Private Bishop already knows who you are, I'll have him serve as a messenger between us. He is a steady man from a good family and I have complete trust I him."

"Sir, I already have a room at the St. Charles hotel."

"Well, they have seen you there in uniform. I suggest that you check out, find a place to change into your civilian duds, and take a room at Mrs. Tolbert's."

"Yes, Sir, will do."

George checked out of his room at the St. Charles and walked out to the edge of town. In a thicket, he changed his clothes. He then folded his uniform and placed it at the bottom of his valise next to a small packet of Jenny's letters, which were carefully tied with one of her hair ribbons. The soft brown leather bag had been a graduation gift from his parents. It was one of the few personal possessions that he had brought west with him.

As he finished what little packing he had to do, he heard the creak and clatter of a wagon outside the thicket. Private Bishop stepped down from the seat and saluted George. George said, "Private, I'm out of uniform now and on a special mission. Let's do away with saluting and other military decorum. From now on, I'm George Dawson, a mining engineer from Colorado. I see that you were told to remove the canvas top from the wagon. And, you have acquired a team without the big 'U.S.' brand on their hips. Good man! It would not do for me to be driving around in a wagon with the Company insignia painted on the canvas or a team of Army horses."

"Yes, Sir, Lieutenant, I mean, George, the Captain told me to remove it and bring the wagon to you. Also, he suggested that we leave messages for each other at the Post Office over on Carson Street."

Private Bishop mounted the horse that had been tied to the back of the wagon. "Good luck, George, I'm due back at the camp." He gave a little wave and spurred the horse out of the thicket and set off to the south.

George climbed up onto the wagon seat and unwrapped the reins from the brake handle. He released the brake and gave the reins a flip to get the team moving. Then, he drove into town and pulled up in front of Benton's Livery. As he stepped down into the dusty street, a man came out to meet him. The man said, "Howdy, they call me Gus. What can I do for you?"

"I'd like to leave my wagon and team with you for a few days while I do a little business here in town."

Gus said, "The wagon yard's around back. Go around the corner yonder and you'll see it. Pull in and I'll meet you back there."

After the wagon was parked and the team unhitched and moved into stalls, George said, "I need to have some shipping crates built to hold mining equipment that I'll be sending by rail back to Colorado. Can you recommend anyone who can build them?"

"Well, there's two or three outfits what does that kinda work but I'd recommend Jack Turner. He'll build 'em stout and give you a fair price. His shop's over near the rail station. Anybody over yonder can point him out to you."

"Thanks, and can you point me to Mrs. Tolbert's boarding house?"

★★★

Mrs. Tolbert rented him a room on the second floor overlooking the street. She said, "Once you get your things stashed in your room come back down to the dining room. We'll be serving a light noon meal in about thirty minutes. And, ever'body calls me Katy. That Mrs. Tolbert stuff has me looking for my Ma."

After a bowl of thin soup and a slice of coarse bread, George walked down the street to Jack Turner's shop. The shop smelled of fresh sawn lumber. Coffins and partially finished cabinets were stacked haphazardly along the walls. A burly, bare-chested man with a mop of auburn hair was smoothing a piece of lumber with a rasp. George said, "Hello, I'm looking for Mr. Jack Turner."

"I'm Jack," said the man, "and don't nobody calls me Mister. What can I do you for?"

"I'm George Dawson and I need to have four shipping crates built to hold tools I am taking back to our mine in Colorado. I've written out the specifications on this sheet of paper. Do you think you can do this and have them ready in a few days?" George handed the paper with the specifications to Turner.

"Yepper, I can build 'em quick enough, say six or seven days since I got these other jobs ahead of you. My helper is off to the rail yard making a delivery but I'll get him sawing the lumber directly he returns. Check back the day after tomorrow and see where we are. We might just get 'em done early."

"Thanks, I'll see you then."

George then went to the lumberyard and ordered what he needed for the false bottoms of the crates. At the mercantile, he selected the tools and nails he would need. The clerk said, "Stranger, you fixin' to do a bit of carpenterin'?"

"Yes," said George, "I've got some bad boards in the floor of my wagon that I need to fix. I have just come from the lumberyard and ordered the little dab of lumber that I need from them. Also, I need to buy some mining tools to ship back to my partners in Colorado. Do you sell mining tools?"

"Yes, sir," said the clerk, "What we don't have in stock,

we order from our supplier over in California. They got ever'thing. What with the telegraph and railroad, we can get stuff in a week or less. By the way, my name is Thomas Wright but ever'body calls me Tommy."

George pulled a folded sheet of paper out of his shirt pocket and said, "Good, Tommy. My name's George Dawson. I'm glad to do business with you. Here's a list of what I need; work up a price for me. I'm staying at Mrs. Tolbert's boarding house. Once you have the prices worked up, contact me there and I'll come finalize the order. Can you hold these hand tools and nails for me until the lumber and mining equipment are here?"

"That won't be no problem. I'll set 'em back here in a bin and put your name on 'em. It were Mr. Dawson, right?"

"That's correct but you can call me George, if you like. Thanks for your help."

Back in his room, George penned a short note to Captain Hamilton giving him an update using their agreed upon code words. The note would not make much sense to anyone else if it were intercepted. After sealing the note in an envelope, George dropped it off at the Post Office to be placed in the military mailbox.

Six days later, a young boy knocked at the door to George's room. George opened the door and said, "What may I do for you, young fellow?"

The boy removed his tattered cap and uncovered a shock of straw colored hair. He looked up at George and said, "Sir, are you Mr. Dawson?"

"Yes, why do you ask?"

"Mr. Turner sent me over here to tell you that your crates are ready, and he wants to know when you can pick them up."

George gave the boy a dime and said, "Tell Mr. Turner that I'll be over to his shop with my wagon in an hour or so."

George penned another letter to Captain Hamilton requesting that the gold be picked up from the Mint and brought to the agreed upon transfer spot east of town. He took the note to the Post Office and then stopped by the mercantile to pick up his nails and hand tools on the way to the lumberyard and Turner's shop.

"Hello, Tommy," George said to the clerk. "I've come to pick those hand tools and nails from you. I'm ready to patch my wagon."

"I've got some good news for you, George. Your mining tools come in this mornin'. Do you want them now?"

"I'll pick them up tomorrow, if that's okay. I have to pick up some crates from Mr. Turner and repair my wagon first. I'm on my way to Turner's shop right now."

"No problem," said Tommy. I'll see you in the morning."

George walked next door to the livery, paid Gus for the livery charges, and hitched his team to the wagon. At the lumberyard, he placed the lumber he had purchased in the bottom of the wagon. Then, he drove to Turner's shop to collect the crates. Once the crates had been loaded, George drove to a little grove of cottonwoods along the river east of town. Captain Hamilton had chosen this secluded spot for the transfer. In two hours, George had built false bottoms and trays for the gold in each of the crates.

Late that night under a quarter moon, Captain Hamilton rode in leading two pack mules. He whistled and George replied from the shadows of the dense brush where he had waited with his team and wagon. They quickly transferred the gold coins to the trays that George had fashioned in the bottom of each crate. They nailed on the lids to the false bottom compartments. George then rubbed dirt and ashes across the new lumber to further disguise the lids on the false bottoms. Both Captain Hamilton and George were satisfied that only a very discerning eye would detect them. The Captain bid George *adieu* and left by way of a different path.

The next morning, George drove the wagon up to the

mercantile and had the mining tools loaded into the crates. He nailed the lids onto the crates where any watchful eyes could see him do it. At the rail station, George had shipping labels made out and attached to the crates and watched, as they were loaded into a boxcar. He left the empty wagon with Private Bishop who drove it off down the street.

The eastbound freight train had a mail car, a flat car loaded with farm equipment, and four boxcars. One passenger car and a caboose were coupled at the end. George took a forward facing seat near the rear of the passenger car. He and Captain Hamilton had decided to forego a military escort on the train, as it would likely draw too much attention. George had his sidearm holstered on his hip as well as a pocket revolver secreted under his left armpit. His jacket helped to conceal it.

Well, just a few days to Ogden, then catch the east bound to Cheyenne. After that, a few hours down to Denver, thought George. *If all goes well, this will just be a long uncomfortable ride.*

XIII

The Wyoming Territory of 1870s was in turmoil. The U.S. Army was involved in a number of battles with the Sioux, Northern Cheyennes, and Arapahos. Civilian law enforcement was spotty and often ended at the town limits of a given local sheriff or town marshal. Cowboys on drunken sprees, gamblers, fights over whores, and petty theft accounted for most of the local lawmen's work. Cattle rustlers and disputes between large cattle operators and small ones occasionally led to a killing or two. The U.S. Marshal service had a presence but they were grossly understaffed and spread too thin for such a large expanse of land.

George was slumped against the window and had been deeply asleep when he was awakened by the sound of gunfire. The train had stopped in a narrow canyon a few miles east of the Green River in western Wyoming. He suddenly realized that the train was being robbed. *My God, they're after the gold*, he thought. He stuck his head out of the window and looked forward. Six masked horsemen were along side the mail car. The leader pulled himself out of the saddle by the handrail next to the mail car door. He fired a couple of shots at the door lock and then slid open the door. George fired a few shots at the waiting bandits with his revolver and hit at least two of them, but they remained in their saddles as they and the other three horsemen whirled away into the brush. Then the outlaws began a steady fire at the passenger car. George and the three other passengers quickly moved away from the near side windows to the far side of the car.

One of the passengers was a big, bearded, scruffy looking fellow dressed in well-worn leather. He reached up into the overhead luggage rack and pulled down a buckskin gun case, which was heavily adorned with leather fringe and Indian beadwork.

"I'm a buffalo hunter by trade," said the man. "My name's Jim Tugmon but folks just call me Tug. This here 45/70 Sharps oughter bust through that brush and flush them shooters out."

He then reached back up to the luggage rack and dragged down a big leather pouch. He extracted an ammo belt loaded with the heavy 45/70 rounds. Tug cracked down the lever on the Sharps and dropped in a round. He eased over to the window at the rear of the car and poked the barrel of his gun out. Wood splintered just above his head and a puff of smoke from the brush identified the location of the shooter. The buffalo gun roared quickly followed by a scream from the brush. A riderless horse burst from the thicket and ran along side the train.

"One down," said Tug. He then shouted, "Who's next?"

U.S. Deputy Marshal Blue Nall was on the trail of six men who had robbed the mine payroll at Rock Springs. Nall was known in Wyoming as "Uncle Sam's One-Man Army". Eight years earlier, Blue was town Marshal in Medicine Bow when he was wounded during a gun battle with three outlaws. He took a bullet in the shoulder when his six-shooter clicked on empty. He swore that he would never be out gunned again. Nall wore a Colt Peacemaker on his hip and had two more mounted either side of his saddle horn. He had a pocket pistol holstered under his left arm, an old Colt .44 stuck in his belt across his belly, and a second pocket pistol stuck in his left boot top. A Winchester lever-action rifle was sheathed in a scabbard under his right leg and a double-barreled scattergun in a scabbard under his left leg.

His brother, Tom, had once laughed at him and said, "Brother, I don't see how you walk with all that hardware hangin' off you."

"Lethally," replied Blue.

Nall was nodding in the saddle as he followed the tracks of his quarry west. He heard shots in the canyon ahead where the railroad tracks disappeared around a bend. Now fully alert, he put spurs to his blue roan gelding. He circled around a hill and rode hard to the west so as to turn around and come at the train from the rear. In five minutes, his horse was sliding and hopping down a loose slope on the south side of the shallow canyon. When he broke into the open, he was around a bend and a quarter mile behind the train. He eased along the train tracks at a lope. The boom of a big bore buffalo gun and a scream from the brush ahead and to his right caused him to stop. He dismounted and tightened his saddle cinch and loosened the leather whangs that secured the scattergun and Winchester. He thumbed the hammer thong off of the Peacemaker and loosened it in the holster. Blue remounted and gave a Comanche yell. Then, he charged at full gallop into the brush where the bandits were hiding.

"Lord, God Amighty," said Tug, "I do believe hell has come to Georgia! Would you listen to all that shootin'. Who is that feller what come a-barrelin' up from behind us? He went past me like a shot out of a Yankee cannon."

Riderless horses burst from the thicket like a covey of quail. Powder smoke hung in the air like thick fog. The gang leader jumped down from the mail car and caught one of the fleeing horses. Just as he swung into the saddle, Tug's buffalo gun boomed. "That's two fer my tally," said Tug.

Blue Nall walked the roan out of the brush and headed

back to the passenger car. He was leading one of the bandits' horses. He shouted, "Don't you boys shoot. I'm U.S. Deputy Marshal and I reckon we got 'em all. There ain't none left to hang. Anybody on the train hurt?"

George stepped down from the car and said, "Marshal, we're all okay. And, we are certainly glad you showed up when you did."

"I've been trailin' that bunch from Rock Springs where they robbed a payroll. I'd be obliged if you could help me catch up these fellers' ponies. I doubt they have run far and there should be five of them back yonder ways. I expect the mine payroll is in one or more of the saddle bags."

It took less than thirty minutes to locate the horses and lead them back to the train. Marshal Nall gathered the train staff, George, and Tugmon next to one of the boxcars.

"Boys, will you help me load these dead bodies into that boxcar? You can off load them at Rock Springs. I'll follow along with the horses and see to the burials when I get there. The mining company posted a reward for the return of the payroll in these saddlebags. Leave contact information with the Depot Agent and I'll see that you boys each get a share of the reward."

George pulled Nall aside and whispered, "Marshal, I'm a military officer traveling in disguise on a special mission. I'll leave my name with the Depot Agent but I cannot and will not accept any of the reward money. You split my share amongst the others or use it as you see fit. I am George Dawson."

"Okay, podner, I'll see to it."

The passengers and train crew used axes to clear the trees that the bandits had felled across the tracks and then loaded the dead bodies into the boxcar. As the locomotive chugged back up to speed, George settled into his seat in the passenger car. *Well, I guess the bandits were not after the gold and had no knowledge of it since they were trying to rob the mail car and not the boxcar. I hope that's the end of excitement until I get these crates to Denver.*

A six-man escort met George at the rail station in Cheyenne. The crates marked 'Mining Tools' were loaded into a boxcar of the train heading south to Denver. Two of the troopers rode in the car with the crates while the other four rode with George in the passenger car. The trip to Denver was uneventful.

San Saba Gold

XIV

Buck tossed his tin plate into the wreck pan beside the chuck wagon. He stepped over to where Sergeant Brown was examining a cattle hide with Ranger Baker.

"Is that another hide from stolen cattle?" asked Buck.

Sergeant Brown turned to Buck and said, "Yepper, Baker brought it down from Mason to see if it was from down here. You can kinda make out part of a brand where somebody tried to burn the hide. The Major's taken an interest in cattle thieves what're selling hides. 'Sides, I overheard him and Captain Coldwell talkin' about a problem with hide thieves stealin' cattle up yonder way."

"That sounds familiar," said Buck. A few months ago, I was on a scout where we trailed a rustled herd that we thought had been taken by Indians but turned out to be hide thieves tryin' to make us think they were Indians. I trailed 'em to Mason where they sold the hides to a tanner there. The tanner, a feller named Hooper, said the men who sold him the green hides said they were from Frio City. We looked into it down in that country but came up empty."

"Buck, I reckon the Major would be interested in hearin' about it. Why don't you ease up along side of him and tell about your scout."

Major Jones looked over at Buck and asked, "Yes, what is it, Sergeant?"

"Sir, I was tellin' Sergeant Brown about a scout I was on back in June where we set out trailin' some Indians that stole cattle and killed a *vaquero*. But it turned out not to be Indians. The thieves were white hide thieves who sold the hides up in

Mason."

"Yes, I read a brief mention of the incident in Lieutenant Coldwell's monthly report but did not know that you had been on that scout or anything about Indians. Why did you think you were tracking Indians?"

"Well, the Dutchman who owned the cattle told us that his man was shot full of arrows. That and the tracks we found were unshod ponies. We finally figured out that they weren't Indians and I guessed that they were just tryin' to keep the Dutchman from followin' by scarin' him off."

"Thank you, Sergeant, I appreciate the details. I have seen other reports from the Border country of whites masquerading as Indians to cover their thievery but not up in this country. You can confirm to Sergeant Brown that we are headed to Menardville and are in search of hide thieves but more of the undisguised kind. He's probably figured most of this out for himself already. I can't keep him fooled for long."

Buck thought he almost saw a smile from Major Jones who was notoriously a man of no humor. Buck slowed his pony until he fell back alongside Sergeant Brown. "He was interested,' said Buck, "but he said, like you guessed, we're lookin' for regular hide thieves this trip."

The Rangers made camp just outside of the German village of Fredericksburg that afternoon. While Buck was organizing the camp, Major Jones took Sergeant Brown and two men with him to visit the town so that he could check for any mail and also gather some fresh provisions for the escort. He had told the men in camp to make ready to leave for Menardville the next morning.

On his return from Fredericksburg, Major Jones summoned Buck to his tent. Buck walked over to the Major's tent and announced his arrival. The Major stepped out and said, "Buck, come walk with me a bit."

They walked along the creek away from the campfire and

out of the hearing of the other Rangers. "Buck, I'm asking you to volunteer for a ticklish mission. As far as the others are to know, you will have reached the end of your current enlistment and have decided to leave the Ranger service. Except for your size and blue eyes, your skin color and facial features are such that I think you could pass for an Indian if you dressed the part and let your hair grow."

"Sir, I have not made this known since joining the Rangers but my mother was a full-blood Choctaw. I'd appreciate it if you kept that information to yourself given the way most Texans and most Rangers feel about Indians."

"Excellent! Of course, I will keep your family history between us. Here is what I have in mind. These hide thieves and cattle rustlers have grown bold. We are spread too thin to catch the craftier of them. Since you are now our expert on cattle brands, I would like for you to pose as an outlaw and see if you can join up with the band that is trying to shift the blame on Indians. Remember that you'll be hunted by your fellow Rangers, by cowmen, and if your ruse is discovered, by the outlaws as well. I want you to think about this between now and when we reach Menardville before giving me your answer."

"I'll sleep on it, Sir, and give you my answer when we get to Menardville. That should be three or four days depending on how hard we push. Plenty of time for me to decide."

The Rangers made camp on the San Saba River just northwest of Menardville. Sergeant Brown and Ranger Harper pulled into camp trailing a couple of mules loaded with provisions that they had picked up in town. While several of the Rangers helped Harper with the unloading, Sergeant Brown walked to Major Jones' tent to deliver the mail.

In a few minutes, Major Jones said, "Sergeant, muster the men. I've got an announcement to make."

In ten minutes, the men with the exception of the camp

cook and his helper, milled about in the open area in front of Major Jones' tent. The Major stepped out and raised his hand asking for quiet.

He held up a letter and said, "Men, I have just received this dispatch from the Adjutant General. The legislature has cut our funding again and frozen our account. I will be forced to decrease the size of each company as well as my own escort. Some of you are nearing the end of your enlistment period. I would like to ask for volunteers first before I have to dismiss any men who want to continue to serve. Do I have any volunteers?"

The men looked at one another and most avoided eye contact with the Major. Finally, Buck raised his hand as did three others. Buck stepped forward and said, "Major, seein' as we ain't been paid for the last three months and it don't seem likely that we'll get paid this month, I think I've done my duty and had enough."

"Thanks, Sergeant McDougal. That's one, I need at least two more. You three that raised your hands decide among yourselves who stays and who goes. If all three decide to muster out, so much the better. Let me know of your decision by morning.

"Men, get back to whatever you were doing. You are dismissed. Sergeant McDougal, follow me to my tent and we'll complete the necessary paperwork."

Buck held the tent flap open and allowed the Major to enter before he stepped inside. The Major sat at his small writing desk and began signing a document. "Sign here, Sergeant McDougal," he said in a loud voice. Then he whispered, "Buck, do you remember that big boulder near where the Llano and Colorado Rivers meet?"

"Yes, sir," whispered Buck.

"Buck, there is a small hole about four feet up in the rock wall just north of that boulder. I'll hide a small box in that hole and it can serve as our post office. In case it gets discovered, we'll need to communicate in code. Any time you leave something to me, address me as Jacob, my grandfather's name. Also, you can send a letter from any post office to Jacob Jones, General Delivery in Kerrville. Or, you can send it to General Delivery in Austin. The Adjutant's Office checks that every day. What should I call you?"

"How's about Mike? That was our mule's name on our farm in Tennessee."

"Good! Why don't you head out west toward Fort Concho? Spend a couple of months out there to let your hair grow and give you a chance to build a reputation as a shady character. Here's two hundred in Yankee silver to stake you. After that you'll have to make your own way. When this is over, I'll do my best to make up whatever you spend beyond the two hundred and for your pay. I have sent a letter to the Adjutant General informing him of your role in this. He is very keen to get this cattle rustling at an end. The cattle trail to Dodge City has opened up again and beef is valuable once more."

Right after breakfast, Buck said his goodbyes, saddled his bay, and packed his belongings on his mule. He rode off toward Menardville leading Patch behind him. He stopped at the livery in town and, after a bit of haggling, sold the gelding and mule to the liveryman. He tied his war bag behind his saddle and rode Patch west following the San Saba River.

Buck took his time and spent two easy days following the river to the little town about a mile north of Fort McKavett. Most folks still called the place Scabtown even though the locals had renamed it Fort McKavett a few years earlier. As Buck rode into town, he decided that the old town name was a pretty good fit. A few soldiers sat on a bench outside one of the saloons. Whores waved at him from the windows on the second floor. Faded paint on the weathered boards above the door declared the place to be named Mable's. Across, on the east side of the street, stood an equally rundown looking saloon bearing a sign proclaiming 'Beer'.

Since Mable's afforded shade from the midafternoon sun, Buck hitched Patch there. He nodded to the soldiers and stepped into the gloom of the saloon. The place reeked of stale beer, tobacco, and cheap perfume. Three rough looking characters and what Buck judged to be a professional gambler were playing cards at a table in the back of the room. A scantily dressed but brightly painted whore was draped over the back of the gambler. Another was standing at the far end of the bar. She started toward Buck as he addressed the bartender, "What you got that's wet and cold?"

"Ain't nothin' cold here 'cept Mable's heart. But, I got some St. Louie beer that's cool."

The bartender had on a little derby hat and a dirty white shirt with the sleeves rolled up to his elbows. He wore a black leather belt and a pair of red suspenders on his striped pants.

Buck thought, *I don't have much use for a feller who can't trust his belt to keep his britches up.* But he said, "I'll try your St. Louie beer and a glass of fresh water."

By that time the whore had sidled up next to Buck, introduced herself as Doris, and asked, "Say, handsome, don't you want to buy me a little drink?"

Buck downed the water thirstily and took a sip of the beer. It just barely made the level of cool. He turned to Doris and said, "Darlin', I'm outta of work and just spent my last nickel on this sorry mug of beer. I reckon you'd do better havin' them card playin' *hombres* satisfy your thirst. Looks like they got money to burn since they're letting that cardsharp with the green swaller-tailed coat cheat 'em out of their cash."

The gambler whirled around so quickly that his whore was knocked to the floor. He held a two-shot derringer in his right hand and said, "Who are you calling a cheat? I run a fair game." He aimed the little gun in Buck's direction.

"I could see you dealin' from the bottom of the deck from way over here," replied Buck. "I figure it's nigh to thirty feet from you to me. If you think you can hit me with that little popgun before I can put a forty-five slug through you, have at it. You've got two shots and less than a half second. To be fair, I'll give you warnin' that the last feller that pulled a gun on me is buried back in San Saba."

Of course, it was all bluff. Buck had never shot anyone in San Saba and he could see that the gambler's hand was shaking. Plus, the little gun wasn't even cocked. Buck heard a noise behind him and said, "Barkeep, I'd put my hands up on that bar if'n I was you. You lied about the beer and I just as soon shoot you for that if you rile me any more. Get around here where I can keep an eye on you."

The three card players jumped to their feet and drew their revolvers. All were pointed at the gambler. One of them said, "All right, you tinhorn, we want our money back and drop that peashooter."

A large, middle-aged woman came part way down the stairs from the second floor. Her hair was dyed a shade of red unknown to natural hair. She had on a blue velvet dress with a low-cut neckline revealing a substantial portion of her breasts. She said, "Duke, give them their money and clear out. I can deal cards until we get us a new dealer."

To Buck, she said, "Stranger, I like your sand. How'd you like a job here to keep the peace? We ain't got no Sheriff in this fleabag of a town, and I sure could use somebody who can keep his head if things need calming. I don't want my place shot up, and I don't want no cheatin' of my customers. I'll pay you forty a month and room and board. I've got an empty room upstairs you can use."

"I'll sleep on it," said Buck as he headed for the door. He mounted his pony and rode upriver for a mile or so before picking a spot to make camp. Early the next morning, he shot a deer, which he carefully skinned. Besides the meat, he wanted the skin to tan in order to make himself some buckskin clothing. It would take another hide or two to make both a pair of pants and a shirt. While a thick venison steak was frying in his skillet, he scraped the underside of the hide with his knife and then pegged it hair-side down out in the sun.

Buck carefully collected as much sinew as he could.

He also trimmed the ragged edges of the hide. He would process both items further that night. He planned to make hide glue from some of the skin and a bowstring from the sinew.

That night Buck piled dead cedar on the fire to make a big pile of ashes. He would need the ashes to remove the hair from the deer hide.

After a breakfast of coffee and bacon, he tied the hide in a tight bundle and hung it with a leather whang from a tree branch to keep the ants and varmints off of it until he returned.

Back in town at the mercantile, Buck traded a hindquarter from the deer for an empty nail keg and a five-pound sack of salt. He left town riding downriver before making a big circle back to his camp upriver. After soaking the nail keg in the river to tighten up the staves, he put in the deer hide and a large quantity of the ashes. He filled the keg with water to make lye from the ashes and placed a heavy chunk of limestone on top of the hide to keep it submerged. After soaking in the lye solution for two or three days the hair could be easily scraped off.

Buck spent the next several weeks hunting and preparing his hides. He had rubbed deer brains and tallow into the hides to made them supple, followed by a goodly rub with salt to help preserve them. He made a bowstring from the sinew and boiled the hide scraps in lye and then in water to make glue. He dried the glue and placed it, the bowstring, and the leftover sinew in a small pouch he had made from a deer scrotum.

While out for a walk along the river one morning, he heard what sounded like a woman singing far upstream. He saddled his pony and rode off to see who it might be. As he topped a little rise, he could see wood smoke down in a little bend of the river. The singing was coming from that direction, and now that he was closer, he could tell that it was a woman singing in an Indian dialect that was unfamiliar to him. Buck reined up two hundred yards from the camp and shouted, "Hello, the camp. I come in peace."

The singing stopped abruptly and a tall, thin man stepped out from behind a tree. He held a big bore Sharps buffalo gun. He was dressed head to foot in buckskins, including knee-high fringed moccasins. "Who be ye and what do you want?"

"My name's Mike Harvey. I saw your smoke and thought I heard a woman singing. I mean you no harm. I'm camped downriver from you a couple of miles."

The man lowered the rifle a bit and said, "Ride on in and have a sit down. My woman's got a pot o' coffee bilin' if'n you want a cup."

Buck swung down from the saddle and tied his pony to a little sumac. "I'd appreciate a cup. Please, ma'am, I liked your song, but I did not recognize the language. I'm half Choctaw myself but our folks are from back east."

The woman bowed her head and smiled. The man spoke up and said, "She's Shoshone and her name's Willow. I'm Fred Miller but folks call me Trapper 'cuz that's what I am."

"Did Willow make your buckskins?" asked Buck.

"Yepper, she's a right smart hand with a bone awl and needle. Why do you ask?"

"I'd like a set for me to wear and I got some hides ready to cut and sew. I was going to have a lash at it myself but I'm no hand at sewing. I'd be glad to pay you whatever you think is fair in cash money if she would consider making me an outfit."

Trapper looked over at Willow and she nodded. "Looks like we can make a deal. Why don't you move your camp up here near us? I've got a trap line set out and will be hunting and trapping here for a week or two."

A few weeks later just before sunset, a shaggy-haired, buckskinned desperado rode into the little town of San Angela just across the river from Fort Concho. He looked Indian except for his blue eyes. He tied a big paint stallion up to the hitching rail outside a rundown cantina.

Buck took a corner table at the back of the cantina. As his eyes adjusted to the dark, smoky room, he saw three men sitting at a table to the left of the front door. They were arguing about something but their voices were low enough to prevent Buck from overhearing.

A young Mexican woman asked Buck, "*Señor*, food or drink?"

"Food and drink," answered Buck.

"Today, we have *pozole rojo con pollo* freshly made. Would you like that?"

"Yes, and coffee to drink, *por favor.*"

Buck found the spicy stew to be excellent and a surprise given the shabbiness of the cantina.

One of the three men at the front table stood up and walked unsteadily over to Buck's table. He reeked of cheap whiskey and sweat. He said gruffly, "What're you looking at, Injun? I didn't know they allowed your type in here."

Buck placed his spoon in his bowl of *pozole* and looked up at the man. He said, "Appears to me I'm looking at a drunk."

The man reached for the revolver on his hip but stopped short of pulling it when he saw the end of Buck's forty-five pointed directly between his eyes. "You best go back and argue with your *compadres* some more afore somebody gets hurt," said Buck. "My business is my own. I 'spect yours is as well. Where I look or don't look is none of your lookout. Leave me be so's I can enjoy my hominy stew."

"Jesse, come on back over here. We don't need no trouble and that Injun ain't botherin' us," said one of Jesse's partners.

The Mexican girl returned with the coffee pot and refilled Buck's cup. She whispered, "Please be careful, *Señor.* They are very bad men. My father says that they are outlaws who steal cattle and have killed several of our people. The soldiers do nothing to protect us from such men. They tell us that they are here to protect the mail coaches and not to serve as our policemen."

Buck thanked the girl and paid for his meal. He stepped out into the street and mounted his pony. He rode down the dusty street and pulled up in front of the livery. After arranging for a stall and some grain for Patch, he took his rifle and bedroll out to the wagon yard, made his bed, and stretched out. A few hours later, he was awakened from a deep sleep by the sound of several pistol shots followed by a blast from a shotgun. He sat up and grabbed his rifle from where it lay beside him. In the bright moonlight, Buck saw three men on horses gallop by. One of the men was bent over his horse's neck. He was obviously wounded.

Someone was shouting back towards the cantina. "Thieves! They have robbed me! Help! Catch them!"

Buck lay back in his bedroll. He thought, *It's damn hard not to be a lawman after all this time as a Ranger but I best lie low and let this hand play out. Come mornin', I'll see if I can trail these owl hoots and join up with them. That might be a way to get into this cattle stealin' operation.*

San Saba Gold

XV

Becky sat on the front porch swing and read from Buck's latest letter. It was a bit hard to read because Buck had used a piece of brown, grease-stained paper bag for stationary and his pencil had smeared in a few places.

Becky said, "Momma, Buck's been mustered out of the Rangers and doing a bit of work for the Major. He says that he won't be writing for a spell but plans to come up this way for a visit as soon as he can. He also says that I should ignore anything bad I hear about him. He says that he will explain it all when he gets up here."

Mrs. Griffin said, "That's nice, Dear. Do you reckon that Buck will ever settle down? There's a right smart of young men around here any one of whom who would make you a good husband. Take for instance, Johnny Wilson. He's town Marshal in Durant Station and good looking to boot. He's honest, fair, and comes from a good Choctaw family. I've seen him watch you walk down the road, and he had the look of a boy who's sweet on you."

"Oh, Momma, Johnny and I went to school together. Don't you know that he has his heart set on my cousin, Sue Capers? They've been sitting together in church for nigh on to a year now. I expect they'll get married come Spring. I heard Johnny's Papa tell Dad that Johnny has been saving every penny to build a house. In fact, he's already bought a piece of land and started on a foundation. You know that a young man doesn't plan to build a house just for himself. Besides, I am certain that Buck will come up here and marry me once he feels that he has met his obligation to the Rangers. Buck gives his word and sticks to it. You've got to know that. Look what he went through to rescue me and to avenge James's murder."

"Well, just don't wait on him forever. Life has a way of slipping on by a person. And, I surely do want some grandchildren to spoil. Now, put your letter away and come help me get dinner on the table. Your Papa and brothers will be coming in from the fields and they'll be hungrier than a pack of bears coming out of hibernation."

A few weeks later, Becky drove the family buggy up to the front of the house. She had gone to Luke's store to buy a sack of flour, some air tights of tomatoes, and a list of other items Mrs. Griffin had asked for. She called out, "Momma, I'm back and I've got news."

Mrs. Griffin stepped out of the front door and asked, "What kinda news? And, did you get that spool of blue thread?"

"Yes, Momma, I got everything on your list including the thread. Luke said that he just got in a new supply of sewing materials, and he thought you might want to stop by and see some of the new fabric that came in. But the big news is that Sue and Johnny have set the date. Sue was there at the store and so excited that she could barely keep still. She asked me to be her matron of honor for the church wedding. I'll need to get sewing right away because the wedding is only three weeks off. They decided not to wait until next spring."

"Well, I won't be surprised if we see a little one born a bit early," said Mrs. Griffin.

"Momma! Don't be saying such things."

Two days later, Becky came into the kitchen and said, "Momma, Sue's grandmother insists on an old style, traditional Choctaw wedding including appropriate courtship. It's a good thing there's a community dance set for this Saturday so that Johnny can throw the pebbles at Sue. You know old Grandma Capers will be watching them like a hawk. They still plan on a church wedding after they have Grandma Capers' wedding."

During the dance, Sue sat along the edge of the meeting hall totally ignoring Johnny. Johnny casually strolled by and tossed a few pebbles at Sue's feet to indicate his intentions toward her. She replied by smiling at him and giving a brief nod. The next day, Johnny's mother met with Sue's mother to determine if she was agreeable to the match. Then, the two women met with the respective heads of their clans to insure that the couple were not closely related by blood. Once these approvals were met, Sue's grandmother set the date.

The wedding was located in a big clearing on a bluff overlooking the Red River. The women of the two extended families set up fires and began cooking for the big feast. Once all preparations were complete, Sue and her friends and young relatives approached the clearing from one direction while Johnny and his group of friends and relatives approached from the opposite direction. As the two groups neared each other, Sue and her contingent took off at a dead run away from Johnny and his group. With much laughter and sham fighting, Johnny eventually captured Sue and brought her to the center of the clearing. The couple sat side-by side. Sue sat down next to Johnny's family and Johnny next to Sue's. Presents were exchanged, speeches given by the elders, and the feast began. Sue's grandmother beamed and seemed completely satisfied.

Sue and Johnny were married again in church the following Saturday. After the ceremony, Johnny said, "Well, I hope everybody is satisfied. We've been married every which way, and I hope nobody comes up with another wedding for us."

Sue said, "Oh, we're good and married for certain."

Mr. Wilson, Johnny's father, drove a decorated buckboard up to the front of the church and invited the couple to climb aboard and have a seat on the bench that had been lashed down in the back of the wagon. Once they were aboard, Mr. Wilson shouted, "Ever'body foller us."

As the wagon topped a little rise, Mr. Wilson said, "You two youngsters quit yer kissin' and look yonder."

Sue stood and turned toward the front of the wagon and gasped, "Look, Johnny, your house is finished!"

"Yepper," said Mr. Wilson, "your families and friends spent all last week building it. Now it's up to you two to make a home of it."

Becky finished up a long letter to Buck detailing all of the recent events. She included a pencil drawing of Buck and herself sitting in a field of flowers. She had always been skillful when it came to drawing and liked to do it. She mailed it in care of Major Jones knowing that he would see that it got to Buck.

XVI

Buck saddled his pony and rode out of town just after first light. He picked up the trail of the three thieves a mile south of town. The wounded one must have been hit pretty hard because there were splotches of blood every few yards in the dust of the road. *That feller ain't likely to last much longer the way he's bleedin',* thought Buck.

The road took a sharp dip down to the ford across the shallow Concho River. The thieves' tracks did not continue up the road south of the ford. *Took to the riverbed to cover their tracks,* thought Buck. *Upstream or down?*

Buck rode a few hundred yards upstream but found no sign that anyone had passed that way. *Not much west of here but the llano estacado. I doubt they would head that way. There'd be no water for a long way once this little river peters out unless they know some of those old Comanche seeps. Ain't likely a group of cattle rustlers would know about them.*

He turned back east and found their trail again a half mile below the ford. They had left the riverbed and turned south across the open country. Buck reined up in a little motte of live oaks and staked his pony so it could graze. He made a lunch of jerky and settled in for a nap. *I reckon I'll give 'em time to feel like nobody is following. They'll likely shade up in a few miles and either tend to their partner's wound or bury him and then make a camp for the evening.*

A couple of hours before sunset, Buck broke camp and saddled his pony. As he topped a little rise, he spotted a brindle bull grazing about a mile off. He used his field glasses to look for others and seeing none concentrated on the lone bull. *Odd for one to be off all by his lonesome this time of year. But I see no sign of a brand. He's likely a maverick that has kept away from whatever rancher works this area or he got run off by a bigger bull. I'll slip around downwind and see if I can throw a loop on him.*

Buck eased around the hill and came at the bull at a dead run. Though the bull was a fast runner, he was no match for Patch who covered the distance quickly. Buck tossed a loop over the bull's horns and dallied him to the saddle horn. As the bull spun to face his adversary, Buck jumped from the saddle and threw a second loop around the bull's hind legs. Back in the saddle, he yanked the second rope tight and spurred Patch away from the bull. The big animal went down in a heap. Quickly, Buck leaped down and tied up the left hind leg to the bull's horns. Thus trussed, the bull could do little but hobble along wherever Patch pulled him.

The bull made a couple of hobbling charges at Buck and Patch before accepting his fate. Buck, Patch, and the bull plodded along for a mile or two before Buck smelled a whiff of wood smoke. *Ah, they're up in that little oak motte ahead,* he thought.

Buck stopped one hundred fifty yards out. Well beyond pistol range and beyond rifle range for all but the most accurate of marksmen. "Hello, the camp," he shouted. "I sure ain't no lawman and I got a suspicion you got a hurt man. I'm coming in with my hands high."

Buck tied Patch to a limb on the outside of the thicket and tied the hobbled bull well away in case the bull made a run at the horse. Then, he stepped from the low brush into the clearing of the outlaws' camp. He held his hands at shoulder level well away from his revolvers.

"Well, if it ain't the Injun we seen back in town. What in the hell do you want and why are you trailing us?"

"I didn't set out to trail you *hombres*, but I couldn't help seein' that blood trail you left. In case you're wonderin', there ain't no posse comin' this a-way and I drug some brush across your tracks for the first few miles outta town. And, I'm only half Injun. You can call me Mike, ever'body else does. Looks like your partner's hurt bad."

"Jesse ain't hurt. He'd dead. We just stopped here long enough to let him go ahead and die. I'm Clayton and the feller over yonder with the gun aimed at you is Zeb. You still ain't said what you want."

"Back at that little cantina I heard that you boys were sorta in the cattle business. I do a bit of that my ownself from time to time. Fact is I got a maverick bull tied out at the edge of this brush. I figger to add a few more to him and drive them south. I know some folks down on the border that buy beeves and take them to some Mexican grandee. They ain't real particular about what brands the cattle carry. You boys are headin' in the right direction so why not partner up. It's a right smart of work for one man to drive a herd off their home ground."

Clayton said, "How's about you go bring in your horse and bull while me and Zeb think over your idea. We didn't get hardly enough money from that cantina to buy a side of bacon. So we might be interested in having you throw in with us for a spell. We'll see."

The bull was grazing on a clump of bluestem when Buck stepped out of the thicket. Patch raised his head from where he was grazing and nickered as Buck approached. Buck lengthened the rope on the bull to allow him more room to graze. He led his horse back into the thicket and tied him to a sapling at the perimeter of the clearing in which Clayton and Zeb were camped.

Buck cleared his throat and said, "I long lined the bull out in the grass where he could graze. What's the verdict, gents? Are we in this together or do I just mosey off on my own?"

Zeb spoke up, "There ain't a whole lot down south of here 'til you reach the border and that's a good hunert and fifty miles over rough, dry country. How you 'spect to put together a herd and not get caught? The ranchers around these parts take rustlin' sorta personal and their *vaqueros* are damn good shots."

"Well, I don't plan to take more than a few from a given spread, and I mean to do most of my work and travellin' at night. The South Concho runs up this way from the south. I reckon there'll be water and grass along it. Once we get to the headwater of it, it's about two to three days southwest to pick up the head of the Devils River. Then, I aim to follow it on down to the Rio Grande."

"Sounds like you've been thinking on this for a spell and have it all worked out," said Clayton. "I reckon me and Zeb will trail along with you for a day or two and see how she goes, but we need to work back to the east where there's more cattle and brush to hide in. This country around here is sorta short on brush taller than a jackrabbit. A feller pushin' beeves across this country is easy to spot from ten miles off."

Buck said, "We've got a full moon tonight, and I plan to head out around midnight. Let's bury your dead partner and get some rest before we set out."

They stopped at daylight and made camp in a bend of the river. Clayton said, "Buck, I doubt we made ten miles. At this rate, we ain't gonna get to the border for weeks. That bull of yours is fightin' near ever' step of the way. If'n we get downwind of another bull or a cow in season, he'll likely break free anyway and maybeso hurt one of us. I say let's kill him and take the hide. What with all the cattle in Texas, the hide is worth as much or more than the live critter. One beef ain't worth the trouble 'til you get him to Kansas or Old Mexico. We can eat some of the meat and eventually sell the hide."

Buck said, "Yep, it was a mistake to try and bring a bull. From here on, we'll stick to steers and cows. We can eat whatever bulls we come across."

After a big breakfast of beefsteak and coffee, they skinned out the bull, rolled up the hide, and tied it onto to Jesse's horse. Zeb had led the dead man's horse behind him.

In rough country, an extra horse was too valuable to leave behind. Since they no longer had the bull in tow, they could ride in daylight without raising undue suspicion should they be observed by some rancher or *vaquero*.

The country south of Fort Concho is dry except along the river. Even the river is intermittent except in the wettest of years. The terrain consists of limestone hills and mesas very sparsely covered with stunted cedars, mesquites, and cacti. Shallow draws and arroyos cut in and around the hills and lead toward the river. The land surrounding the hills is covered with a scattering of low drought hardy brush, cacti, and occasional cedars. It is a hard country for man and his stock. The few ranches are huge due to the scarcity of forage for livestock. In 1876, there was nothing one would designate as a town between Fort Concho and San Felipe del Rio down on the Mexican border. Considering the meandering route needed to follow the rivers, it was a distance of more than one hundred seventy-five miles.

They stopped at mid-morning a few days later to water their horses and fill their canteens at a little trickle of a spring to the side of the dry riverbed. Their progress had been slow due to lack of water and forage for the horses. To lose your horse in this country was a sure death sentence.

Clayton said, "Mike, it's been dry this year and this so called river ain't even had a damp spot for the last two days. We're lucky to chance on this little spring. We ain't seen a steer in three days and ain't likely to. Drinkin' this gyppy water has tore up my insides something terrible. Me and Zeb are heading back to the east. There's cattle just beggin' to be took along the Nueces, and it ain't that far from there on down to Mexico. You can keep headin' south if'n you want to but we're done with it."

"Maybe you're right. I'll trail along with you boys a ways, but I got papers out on me over in Uvalde and I'd just as soon not head that far down on the Nueces."

Buck was known to be a Texas Ranger by the folks in Uvalde. Even though his appearance was greatly changed, he did not want to take the chance that his true identity would be revealed. Besides, this country along the Concho and Devils Rivers was well beyond the Frontier Battalion's normal area of responsibility. It was too sparsely settled and the big ranchers were able to defend themselves. The likelihood of uncovering the identities of bands of rustlers was remote.

"Saddle up, boys," said Clayton. "We've got a long ride from here to the breaks of the Nueces, and we can't push these ponies too hard. Tomorra and the next day are gonna be tough. There's bound to be water in the Nueces, but we ain't likely to find any betwixt here and there."

XVII

Colonel Morris and a troop of his cavalry had been detached to Denver to guard the Mint and to organize the shipment of funds to San Antonio. Colonel Morris took an office on the ground floor of the Mint. For the last week, he had expected to receive Lieutenant Dawson and the gold shipment and was becoming a bit concerned.

There was a knock at the door and then his orderly stuck in his head. "A Lieutenant George Dawson is here to see you, Sir."

Colonel Morris looked up from his desk and said, "Show him in and close the door. Also, slip outside and run anybody off who's slinking around that window. I do not want to be disturbed when Dawson and I meet."

Lieutenant Dawson stepped into the office and snapped a salute to Colonel Morris. "I have brought the shipment intact though there were a few tense moments along the way."

"Good man," said the Colonel. "Now let's plot out a plan and a route to get you to San Antonio. As you know, Washington City is a leaky sieve and word is out that money is being shipped down from here to San Antonio for the new Post. Therefore, I think it best that we not use the normal route. If it were anything else, we would ship by rail to Kansas City and down into Texas by rail and stage line. However, there are too many folks who would be waiting to waylay the shipment along that route. What I propose is that we make an accidental slip that silver is being shipped to San Antonio via Kansas City. I've had my orderly crate up five hundred pounds of lead bars and marked them for shipment to the new Post in San Antonio. He is a man of impeccable loyalty to the service. Only he and I, and now you, know what is in those crates. He is leaving by rail day after tomorrow with a heavy guard detachment. They will place the crates in the mail car under constant guard. A guard will be posted in the engine and in each passenger coach. That should convince everyone that the true shipment in going by rail."

George said, "That sounds good, Sir. And, what about the real shipment?"

"I have two trustworthy Sergeants who worked as freighters before the war. We'll split your gold into two lots and load them into the bottom of wagons full of uniforms, saddles, and tack. The Sergeants will drive the teams, and you will lead a detachment of men as an escort. Only you, me, and the Sergeants will know about the gold."

"Sir, I would request that we outfit the detachment with the new repeaters just in case we run into trouble."

"Lieutenant, I fear that would draw undue attention and make the men of the detachment suspicious. They will be issued standard breech loading Springfields just as they would on any patrol."

Colonel Morris pulled a map from his desk drawer and said, "George, here is the route I want you to take. As you can see, I've had you bypass all of the major towns. Head south from here at the Mint and down to just east of Trinidad. From there, you need to head east a ways to skirt around the mountains, then southeast through a little stretch of New Mexico and into the Texas Panhandle. There is a trading post on the Canadian River right about here near the site of Adobe Walls," he said as he pointed at the map. "You can re-provision there if need be.

"Then, go south by southeast until you reach a little town called Albany. From there you can follow the cattle trail the Texans are calling the Western Trail. The Trail will eventually lead to a town called Kerrville, way down here on the map. The Texas Rangers have a post near there. They can put you on the old San Antonio Road from there. It is a long way, nine hundred to a thousand miles over dry open country much of the way and many rivers to cross down in Texas. I figure you will average about fifteen miles a day. That means a trip of two or, more likely, three months barring bad weather. Get some rest, you leave at sunup."

"Yes, Sir, I'm sure we'll make out fine. But, we will require a water wagon and a freight wagon for tents, cooking gear, grain for the mules and horses, and provisions. Do you have trusted men to drive them?"

"Well, I did not want to send him, but my son is a Corporal with this detachment and he is a fair hand with a team. I will speak with him and swear him to secrecy. He can be your third driver and I'll find you a fourth."

"Thank you, Sir. Also, I'd like some extra wagon wheels strapped onto the load. We are sure to need them. I'm a fair hand as a wheelwright. My grandfather ran a wagon works back in Illinois. We will need a few tools as well."

They were two hours late getting started due to one thing or another, but by midday they were on the road south of town. They camped for the night on the east bank of Cherry Creek, a good six miles from the edge of the city. After everyone had their supper, George summoned his teamsters and scout to his tent.

George unrolled a map and spread it on a table. "Men, I propose that we follow along the creek until in peters out here a tad northeast of Henry's Station. I have heard some of the grumbling and know many think we should have taken the train to Pueblo. The Colonel and I did not want too many folks wondering why the Army was loading wagons onto a train. And, I have overheard questions as to why we are hauling uniforms and tack all this way by wagon when such stuff should be readily available closer to San Antonio. If any of you hear such from the men, tell them that the Army Brass ordered it even if it makes no damn sense. You can hint that the uniforms and tack were sold to the Army in Denver by the brother of a Senator. They should have no trouble believing that!

"I reckon that we will take three days or a bit more to reach the upper end of Cherry Creek. When we get there, we can meet again and map out the next leg of this journey. Now, get some rest. We have a long, hard pull ahead of us."

The first few days were largely a matter of getting the men and animals accustomed to the monotony of the plodding mules. The country was covered in low prairie grasses and the creek supplied water as well as firewood from the cottonwoods that grew along its banks. They were using the old wagon road south. These days most folks used the train or the newer road that ran along side the railroad. Besides himself and his four teamsters, George's command included a scout and eight troopers. Since the road south was obvious, the scout had little to do. He spent his time riding on the lead wagon or out hunting for meat for the camp. Two of the troopers rode a few hundred yards ahead of the wagons and two rode the same distance behind. The other four served as outriders a short distance either side of the wagons. By prearranged signals, the troopers switched positions several times a day. George had them do this to help break up the boredom that was bound to set in. George spent his time riding along with the trooper or troopers at each position to get to know his men better and to anticipate which position might be the easiest to attack.

Since the men had been handpicked by Colonel Morris, there was not a shirker in the group. By the third evening, everyone fell into a routine. Two of the men were excellent camp cooks and readily took over those duties. The others assisted with wood gathering, setting up tents, and the other duties of life on the trail.

Occasionally, they would meet a wagon or a horseman on the road but there was never any evidence of a threat. Besides, most folks gave the Army a wide berth. These westerners were an independent lot and seemed to have little use for the Army except when Indians were around.

George was riding with the troopers out front when the scout, Bill, rode in from the west. "Lieutenant, this little pissant crick is dried up from here south. That hole of water over yonder is the last of it," he said as he pointed toward the line of cottonwoods a mile to the west."

Bill continued, "This here road makes a fork a few miles ahead. One branch heads pertnear due west, likely to Henry's Station. The other wanders off to the east-southeast. Due south there's a bad stretch of hills thick with trees. No way to get these wagons through there. You're going to need to pick your poison. It's either go west and through that little town or go east into the open prairie. There ain't a drop of water out on that plain. There's a big crick just west of Henry's Station that runs south all the way down to the Arkansas River and a good road all the way to Pueblo. We'll run into a passel of more folks that way, but it seems to me the better choice.

"The east route means three or four days with no water but what we tote in them barrels and the water wagon. Fourteen men and two dozen horses and mules will sop up a lot of water in four days. If you choose the east route, I recommend that we travel at night. The stock won't need as much water that way. I can line us out a route so's we don't drive off a cliff or into a prairie dog town. We got a good moon for the next week. Laws, that's more words than I have run together in a month."

"We'll go east of the hills. Between the water wagon and the barrels in the freight wagon, we have enough water for four or five days as long as we are sparing with it," said George. "Lead us on, Bill."

Four days later, a purple-black line of clouds boiled over the mountain range to the west of them. Bill came galloping back from the south waving his hat. As he reined in he panted, "Lieutenant, there's a bad storm a-comin. Best we circle up these wagons and put the stock in the middle. There'll be lightnin' and thunder a-plenty. We don't want to have any of these critters spook and run off. Liable to be some powerful wind, too. Be right smart to lash anything loose down. The good news is that we should get plenty of fresh water in the gullies and *playas*."

"Okay, Bill. Men, let's get these wagons circled up tight and put the horses and mules inside the circle. Set out any barrels, buckets, and such to catch what rainwater we can. Private, climb up on the top of the tank wagon and open up the hatch."

An hour later, the storm hit. The men crawled under to wagons as minie ball sized hail pelted down. The animals were left to suffer their fate. Fortunately the hail only fell for a few minutes but then torrential rain poured. Wind rocked the wagons enough that the men feared, at one point, that they would be overturned. In an hour, the storm moved to the east and the men crawled out to check the horses and mules. Although one of the wagon covers was badly ripped, they had sufficient spare canvas to repair it.

George stood ankle deep in mud as he looked about. He said, "A couple of you men set to sewing up that wagon sheet while the rest of us pour what water we caught into the tank wagon. Bill, saddle up and scout around to see if you can find a catchment where we can top off the wagon and water barrels."

XVIII

Buck said, "Boys, we ought to be able to reach the North Llano River in less than two days. Even in dry years there's water to be found there. There is some rough country to wind through from there on down to the Nueces but we can find water every day. I know that country. It's a steep climb down into the canyons of the Nueces once we get close. Old Lew Barksdale drew in some settlers down there and they call their little town Dixie for an old military camp that used to be nearby. There is a little saloon where we can get a meal and a little forty rod. Also, maybe some information as to who is a little loose in guarding their cattle."

Buck heard the hammer click back to cock on a revolver behind him. Zeb said, "Me and Clayton has been talkin' and figger to haul your Injun hide down to Uvalde and maybeso collect the reward. You done said that they got paper out on you. Keep your hands up where I can see them. Any sudden moves and you're dead."

Clayton said, "We used to do a little work for Lew Barksdale and he tried to hang us just because we was a little free with a heated up D-ring. He shoulda picked a brand that warn't so easy to change. If'n a Blue Norther hadn't blowed in while they was leadin' us to a hangin' tree, we'd a-been done for. As it was, I took a bullet in my laig. It went through me and kilt my horse. I was able to skitter off into a thicket and they give up lookin' for me 'cuz of the sleet. Was my lucky day, I reckon. Anyway, today ain't your lucky day."

They took Buck's weapons and tied his wrists to the saddle horn with a couple of leather whangs. Zeb followed behind while Clayton led Buck's horse.

Buck thought, *if these two get to Uvalde with me or without me, they will discover that there is no reward out for me. That will effectively end my brief work in disguise. Some how, I've got to get loose and eliminate them or at least keep them away from Uvalde.*

★★★

Three days later, they were camped on the West Nueces River a few miles from the little settlement named Whistler. There was good water here and plenty of it. Zeb had managed to shoot a fat whitetail doe. Strips of the meat were sizzling in a cast iron skillet sitting on a bed of glowing mesquite coals. Clayton had dragged Buck out of the saddle and dumped him next a big pecan tree. Buck fell over onto his side and mumbled to himself. The two outlaws had denied water to Buck for the last two days to take the fight out of him even though he had not yet put up any resistance.

While Clayton was watering the horses and Zeb was occupied with the skillet of venison, Buck crawled to the riverbank and tumbled into the shallow stream. He drank deeply and lay in the water allowing it to seep into him. He knew that he should not drink too much, too soon but his thirst was agonizing.

"Zeb, what the hell are you doin'," shouted Clayton. "Where'd that half breed get off to?"

"Hell, I don't know. I thought you was watchin' him. He can't have got far in the shape he's in. Look down by the river. If'n I was him, I'd scrambled down to get water."

Clayton walked over to the tree where he had deposited Buck and could see the drag marks where Buck had crawled to the river. "There he is like you speculated," said Clayton. "Come help me drag him outta there afore he drowns."

Buck took another couple of deep drinks before the outlaws got to him and dragged him back to the pecan tree. Clay took a *riata* and tied Buck to the tree. His hands were still bound by the leather whangs.

While Clayton and Zeb were eating their venison and

drinking coffee, Buck began to revive a bit. Moment by moment his wits were returning. *These whangs got a good soaking*, thought Buck. *One thing about rawhide, it'll stretch a good bit when wet.* Buck spread his wrists as hard as he could. The leather gave a bit and then a bit more. Finally he was able to loosen his left hand enough to free both hands. After biting through the whangs, he wrapped the leather strips back around his wrists with Clayton's knots clearly visible on top but held the loose ends in his clenched left hand.

Clayton came over with a burnt strip of meat and held it where Buck could grab it with his teeth. "Don't want you to die on us yet. We'll kill you if need be but the law likely wants you to stand trial. We wouldn't want to risk that reward, now would we?"

Clayton laughed loudly at his own joke and turned back toward the campfire. He had just poured himself a cup of coffee when a man stepped into camp with a shotgun leveled at Clayton and Zeb.

"Take your left hands and slowly pitch your shooters over here at my feet. Don't try anything funny or you'll be eatin' double-ought buck for your dessert. I see one of you is ridin' my horse and I aim to get him back. You know the penalty for horse stealin', don't you? Two of them other horses have DeLeon brands on them. Those belong to my boss. I reckon you are the ones what took them and twenty head of beef from us three months ago."

Clayton said, "Now, hold on there, podner. We bought them horses off a couple of fellers up at Concho. Ain't that right, Zeb?"

"Yep, that's the gospel," chimed in Zeb.

Buck was hidden from the cowboy's view behind the big pecan tree trunk. He said in a loud voice, "*Compadre*, don't shoot 'em yet. I'm their captive, and they are rustlers and thieves. Don't believe anything they tell you."

Clayton said, "Don't listen to him. We were taking him in to collect a reward."

The cowpoke spoke up, "What'd he do to have a bounty

on him?"

"Well, we don't rightly know but he's wanted for sure."

"Ease over here and put your bellies in the dirt. Stick your hands behind you and tuck them into your belts. You, behind the tree, come out here where I can see you."

Buck dropped the leather bindings from his wrists and freed himself from the *riata* holding him to the tree. "I managed to work myself loose and was waiting for a chance to get away," he said as he stood up and stepped into view. "That paint pony is mine but the other three horses are theirs. The third one is from their dead partner. He was shot while they were robbing a cantina up at the town near Fort Concho. I have no doubt those are stolen horses."

"Why you ain't nothing but a blamed Injun," said the cowboy. "I reckon I'll just hang you, too."

Buck saw no choice but to trust the cowboy. He whispered so that the outlaws could not hear what he had to say. "My name is Caleb McDougal but folks call me Buck. I need to swear you to secrecy before I tell you any more."

"Okay, I swear. So what's you story."

"I'm a Texas Ranger in disguise on a special mission. My pistol belt is hangin over on that limb. There is a little pocket under the buckle. My badge is in there."

"Well, my name is Starcher but ever'body calls me Starch. You tie up these two real tight and remember I've got this scattergun if you or they try anything funny."

Buck walked over to the pecan tree and picked up the *riata* that Clayton had used to tie him to the tree. He walked over to where the outlaws were lying and said, "Get up real slow, Zeb, and put your hands on top of your head."

Buck pulled Zeb's knife out of its sheath and threw it over to where the two revolvers lay in the dirt. He pulled a hideout pistol out of Zeb's right boot and another out from under his shirt. Those he tossed into the dirt as well.

"Now, put your hands back here behind you."

Buck securely tied Zeb's hands and stepped back. He turned to Starch and said, "I need to borrow that knife back to cut off the tail end of this *riata* so's I can truss up Clayton, okay?"

Starch nodded. Buck walked over and picked up the knife. He went back to where Zeb stood and cut the length of the *riata* away from Zeb. He turned to Clayton and said, "Alright, Clayton, your turn. Roll over and ease up here behind your buddy, Zeb."

As Buck bent over to pick up the *riata*, Clayton gave him a shove with his boot while at the same time shoving Zeb toward Starcher. As Buck hit the ground the shotgun boomed. Zeb took one barrel in his chest. He was dead before he hit the ground. He was the lucky one. The second barrel hit Clayton in the belly. He writhed on the ground screaming in agony. It took him two minutes to die and they were hard minutes.

Buck sat up and checked himself. Not a scratch. Starcher dropped the shotgun and exclaimed, "Laws, I kilt a man! No, two of them."

Buck stood up and walked over to him. "You had no choice. They would have killed us both. Are you going to be okay?"

"Give me a minute." After a few minutes, he said, "I wasn't really going to hang them. I would have taken them back to the ranch and let *Señor* DeLeon do it."

"Why don't you help me drag these bodies over here to the river? Since we don't have a shovel to bury them, we can cave in a cut bank over them easy enough. Then we can have some coffee and something to eat. Those outlaws didn't feed me enough over the past few days to keep a frog alive. I'm half starved and there's a venison ham hanging in that tree by the fire."

After they had caved the cut bank over the two bodies and washed up, Buck sliced some venison into the skillet and started a fresh pot of coffee. He said, "Thanks for saving my hide. How'd you happen along here anyway?"

Starch cleared his throat and said, "I was on my way back to the ranch after delivering some horses to a buyer in

Uvalde. I caught a whiff of mesquite smoke and figured that someone was camped here on the river. When I got close, I could see the horses picketed out in that little meadow, and I spied the DeLeon brand on one of the horses. Of course, you know that we waddies have a code of honor to ride for the brand as long as we work for a man. So I tied my pony to a tree and eased close on foot. Once I saw my own horse amongst the others, I knew the horse thieves were here. So I went back to the pony I rode in on, grabbed my scattergun, and threw down of those two. Are you a sure enough Ranger?"

"Yepper, but I'd be real obliged if you would forget about seeing me. The mission is real important to Texas and to cowmen like yourself. Why don't you go bring your pony up with the rest of them while I finish frying up this meat? You and I might as well camp here for the night. Come morning, you can take your stolen stock back to your boss. The big paint is mine. You can have the outlaws' weapons, saddles, and such to sell or whatever you want. I'll keep my gear and this skillet and coffee pot. Also, I'll take the coffee and beans in that sack over there."

Starch surprised Buck when he returned. He was carrying a beautiful guitar. Buck said, "That thing's a beauty. Where did you get it? Mexico?"

"Nope, I built it myself. In the winter when the ranch work is kinda slack, I build fiddles, guitars, mandolins, and such. Folks buy them and that gives me a bit of extra cash. I'm saving up to buy a ranch of my own."

After dinner, Starch played his guitar and sang a number of songs about cowboy life. Buck had heard one or two of them before, but he had never heard them played or sung as well.

"Say, Starch, since you built all these types of wooden things, do you know of any Bois D'Arc trees anywhere in this country?"

"Matter of fact, I do. I sometimes use a little of that wood for the necks of instruments. It's good hard wood and it's got that pretty orange color. There's a feller name of Watkins over on the Frio that planted a grove of them as a sort of fence line. Why do you want to find a Bois D'Arc tree?"

"I want to build a bow and make some arrows. My mother was a full blood Choctaw, and she taught me how when I was just a button. Now and again, I'd rather hunt with a bow than to reveal my location by shooting my rifle."

"Well, It's a long way around to Watkins' place by way of Uvalde to get you back up the Frio. Of course, you could head east from Old Camp Wood but the trail over them little mountains is mighty rough."

"I know the Frio River country pretty good. Patch and I are good at scrambling over rough terrain. I reckon I'll head east come daylight."

San Saba Gold

XIX

The Arkansas River east of Pueblo, Colorado is a shallow meandering stream with a sandy bottom. In many places, quicksand is a major problem for anyone attempting to cross.

Bill rode back to meet George at the head of the procession. "Lieutenant, I've scouted up and down the river east of Pueblo and found a couple of places where I think we can get across. Of course, we can cross easy back in Pueblo, but you said you plan to steer clear of towns."

George said, "Good work, Bill. What are the approaches like on both banks and how solid is the bottom? I have been told that the Arkansas tends to be full of quicksand."

"We need to dig out an approach on both sides but it ought to be easy enough. The banks are mostly sand and gravel. The digging should be easy. The bottom is firm if you keep moving at a reasonable pace. If you bog or stand still, you'll get swallowed up. Unlessen we go through Pueblo or three days west of town to find a rocky bottom, we're just going to have to bust across the best we can. Can you send some of the troopers ahead with picks and shovels so we can get those approaches made? I reckon we'll need the better part of a day to get that work done. By that time, you ought to have the wagons down to the north bank so we can cross. The one that I am really worried about is that water wagon. It is god-awful heavy unless we drain the water. I surely do hate the idea of wasting water out here."

"I'll think on it," said George. "Go ahead and pick out what men and tools you need for building the crossing. I'll ride down there with you to have a look myself and then come back to the wagons."

At the spot Bill had chosen for the crossing, George dismounted and tied the reins of his horse to a bush. The approaches were not a bad as he had anticipated. Although the river had cut the banks, they needed to cut them down only three or four feet to build a sloping ramp that would reach the stretches of sand on either side of the running stream. George estimated that the crossing was maybe one hundred yards from the top of the north bank to the top of the south. The stream of water was only forty yards wide. It was too murky to see the bottom but when Bill rode across, the water did not reach his stirrups. Of a bit more concern to George was the thirty yards or more of loose sand between the high banks and the water on either side. His engineering background might come in handy.

"Bill, once the troopers get the banks cut down to make a reasonable little ramp on either side, help them cut down some of those cottonwoods growing along the edge, trim them up, and drag the trunks and larger limbs down here. We'll build a bit of a wooden road across this loose sand. I will send a trooper back with axes and a bucksaw. Cut the logs and limbs six feet in length and lay them crossways across the sand. If you see that you will run short of enough logs and limbs, space them a foot or two apart and fill in the gaps with cut brush. Here, let me draw you a little picture in the sand of what I have in mind. We made roads like this back in Illinois to get across boggy ground. It should work for us here. If we run short of time, I will make camp here on the north bank for a couple of days until we can get our road built."

Three days later, the wooden road was built and they were ready to cross. Two troopers tied ropes to the front corners of the first wagon and lashed the other ends to the leather straps at the center of their saddles' cantles. George decided to use a four-mule team to pull each wagon across and a six-mule team for the water wagon. The most experienced teamster, Sergeant Sean O'Halloran, took the seat on the first wagon.

George said, "Sergeant, ease across the log road but whip them up when they hit the water. You can rein them back once the wagon is on the logs on the other side, but we don't want to bog in that water bottom. I have waded my horse back and forth a few times and it is okay as long as you keep moving. I stopped my horse midstream for about ten seconds, and he sank up past his fetlocks. So do not delay."

What with crossing and re-crossing the mule teams, it took one and one-half hours to get the first three wagons across and up onto hard ground. They had no real difficulty getting them across.

Next came the heavy water wagon. Even though the tank was only half full of water, George estimated that the wagon and water weighed close to four tons. Those two inch wide iron rims were going to cut deep once they hit the streambed.

While the six-mule team was being hitched and the troopers on horseback were affixing their pull ropes, George said to Sergeant O'Halloran, "What do you think, Sergeant? You got the first three across without bogging. Do you think you can get this heavy wagon across here or should we empty the tank?"

"Well, Sir, I know we have a long way to go across mighty dry country. I tasted the water in this river and it ain't too bad, but it ain't as sweet as what's in that tank. I sure would hate to give up that water, and I believe I can get her acrost. How about we saddle the wheeler mule on the left and have Sergeant Kelly ride him. Between the two privates pulling with their horses, me at the reins, and Kelly on the left wheeler, I reckon we'll do just fine."

"Okay, let's do it."

Sergeant O'Halloran climbed aboard and gave a whistle. As they eased across the near side wooden road, cottonwood logs were popping like pistol shots as the rear wheels broke them. When the lead mules hit the water,

Sergeant O'Halloran popped his bullwhip over the heads of the team and gave a shout, "Go like hell, boys!"

They almost made it to the wooden road on the far side of the stream before the back wheels sank to their hubs. Two of the mules slipped and fell. George shouted, "Okay men, hold up before we kill a mule or injure one of you. Sergeant O'Halloran, hop off and open the tap on the tank. Meanwhile, two more of you get your horses lashed to the wagon tongue and every one pull. We can't let it sink any further."

After the tank drained down to approximately one-quarter full, the rear wheels made a loud sucking sound as the men and animals were able to wrest the wagon up onto the south wooden road.

George shouted, "Shut off that tap and save what water we can."

Sergeant O'Halloran and the men were then able to ease the heavy wagon up onto hard ground south of the river.

Bill rode into camp with a couple of antelope that he had shot. The two camp cooks cut up the meat and began cooking up big pots of stew.

George assembled the troopers said, "Men, the remainder of the day is a holiday. You are free to bathe in the river and wash your uniforms and other clothing. The only thing you need to do first is to fill all canteens, water barrels, and any other empty receptacles with water from the tank wagon. Tomorrow morning after breakfast we will fill up that tank with water from the river. Bill tells me that we have several weeks down to Adobe Walls across dry country. Be especially frugal with your use of water."

That evening, Bill and George sat on the tongue of the water wagon. Bill lit a hand-rolled and said, "Lieutenant, there ain't many landmarks south of here to set a course by. You can use your compass, of course, and steer by the sun, but it is easy to get so you're circling back on yourself out here. We need to head a hair east of due south. There's some rough breaks and canyons along the way that we best go around. I had some of the boys cut me a couple dozen fairly straight poles. I'll tie a rag on the top of each and use them to mark the best way to go. Y'all can pick 'em up as you get to them so's we can use them the next day. That way I can lead you to spots where you can get the wagons across the little canyons and to any water I can find. Wild critters got to drink just like the rest of us, and they leave tracks in this sandy soil. Water may be far apart and hard to find, but we can get across. Also, there are still a few bands of young Comanche and Kiowa bucks that slip off the reservations to cause mischief. Keep your eyes peeled and your weapons handy. The Comanches and Kiowas still think they own this territory even though they're pretty well whipped."

San Saba Gold

XX

Buck saddled Patch and swung aboard. He tipped his hat to Starch and rode across the river toward the breaking dawn. The hills on the east side of the Nueces rose six hundred feet or more above the river canyon. The side canyons often ended in a box barring a man on horseback. Buck followed the river south until he reached the old abandoned Camp Wood. Buck had been on a few scouts through this area with his Ranger troop. He knew a flowing creek ran down to the Nueces approximately six or seven miles downstream of Camp Wood. A faint meandering trail up that creek would eventually lead across the divide to the canyon of the Frio River. Starch had told him that Mr. Watkins and the Bois D'Arc trees were at the little village of Rio Frio.

Patch had an easy gait and Buck dozed a bit as they followed the river south. By mid-morning, they reached the creek flowing out from the side canyon to the east. Buck dismounted and removed Patch's saddle and blanket. He slipped off the bridle and replaced it with a halter to which he attached his *riata*. He tied the end of the *riata* to a cedar and allowed Patch to roll in the caliche dust and shake himself. He filled his canteen with the cool clear creek water and sat in the shade of a pecan tree while Patch grazed on the meadow beside the creek. *This sure is a pretty place,* thought Buck. *It would be a good spot for a little ranch. There's good water and grass enough if a fellow didn't put too many cattle on it.*

Buck awoke with a start. He had dozed off and the noon sun had shifted his shade away from him. His buckskin shirt was sticking to his back with sweat. Patch was standing giving Buck a disgusted look as though he thought Buck had gone *loco*.

Buck stretched and stood up. He said, "Okay Patch, old boy, I reckon you're right. Let's head on to Rio Frio and see this Watkins fellow about a few sticks of wood."

He slung his bridle over his shoulder and picked up the blanket and saddle. "Look at you, Pard. You're covered in that chalky dust."

Buck set his tack back down and walked over to a cedar. He cut off a little branch and used the green cedar needles to give Patch a good brushing. Not only did that get rid of most of the dust but it also left a fragrant smell behind.

"I hope we don't run into any fillies. With you smelling so sweet, we might just have a regular parade following us." Patch did not seem amused, although he did like the brushing.

Once back in the saddle, Buck gigged Patch with his heels and off they set. They were in no hurry. Buck knew that the creek canyon split about five miles in. He needed to take the right hand branch to cross the divide into the Frio River watershed. The meandering creek had cut a half-mile wide canyon through the steep sided limestone hills. The hills were densely covered in cedars. Broken and weathered slabs and boulders were strewn at the foot of the hills. To Texans in this area, these were called mountains but that was local terminology.

Once Buck took the right hand branch of the creek, the going got rough and Buck crossed over to the south side of the creek where the floodplain was a bit broader and not as littered with big rocks.

Patch had just climbed up out of the creek bed when Buck reined him to a halt. *What are all these cattle tracks doin headin east? This canyon boxes up at the end. I'll have to lead Patch on foot up over the hills on a game trail. There's no way to get a herd up over it.*

Buck dismounted and led Patch behind him as he examined the tracks in the dust. Buck flipped a cow patty over with the toe of his moccasin. *That cow patty is still wet enough for those tumble bugs to still be working it. Ain't more than a couple of days old. And these tracks are fresh enough that the wind hasn't blown them out.*

Buck remounted and eased his long gun out of the scabbard. He carried it across his lap where he could bring it into play if need be. He clucked a couple of times and gave Patch a gentle gig with his heels. The Comanche, White Elk, had trained Patch well. The horse readily responded to leg commands, which allowed his rider to keep his hands free of the reins when necessary. Buck applied pressure with his right knee and Patch responded by turning to the left. They stopped when they reached a steep slope on the south side of the canyon. Buck dismounted and dropped the reins to the ground. Patch knew that this was a signal for him to remain standing still until he received another command from Buck.

Buck climbed up the jumble of broken limestone until he could see up the canyon as far as the next bend, which was a quarter mile or so off. No cattle were in sight so he clamored back down and remounted.

He repeated this upon arrival at the next bend in the canyon. As he peeked over a big slab of limestone, he spotted twenty or more steers grazing in a meadow. Someone had built a brush fence across a narrow spot in the canyon effectively penning the cattle. A brief flash of reflected sunlight revealed the location of a guard just beyond the brush fence and above the meadow on the left canyon hillside.

Buck hid Patch in a clump of cedars on the north side of the canyon and scrambled to the top of the hill. In several places, he had to pull himself from cedar to cedar to manage the steep slope. Once he gained the summit, he crept along the ridge until he was above and beyond the spot where the guard was stationed. He sat down behind a low growing cedar and cut off a couple of small branches to allow him a clear view of the guard and the cattle below while remaining well concealed.

After a wait of thirty minutes, he saw movement up canyon from the cattle. Two men rode out on horseback leading a third horse. The guard skittered down from his post to meet them at the brush fence. The guard moved a few branches so that the riders could pass through, then reclosed the gap. The guard mounted and all three headed down canyon at a trot.

Buck gave them thirty minutes before moving. He also wanted to be certain that there was no fourth rider down there with the cattle.

Once he was satisfied that he was alone, he worked his way down to the meadow to have a look at the cattle. He counted twenty-three steers and six different brands. *Got to be rustlers. No legitimate cowman would pen up a herd with this many brands. Anybody moving a legally bought herd would have added a trail brand of his own. Rustlers are generally a lazy lot, elsewise they'd be doing honest work. Too lazy to add a trail brand.*

Buck worked his way around the brush fence and walked back to where he had hidden Patch. He untied his pony and mounted. He rode up to the brush fence and shook out a loop in his *riata*. A well-placed toss snared a big branch of the cedar brush. He backed Patch to pull aside the branch and a few others entangled in it. Another couple of tosses and drags and he had a good-sized gate opened in the brush.

He eased Patch around the cattle, gave a shout, and swung his *riata*. The steers began moving away from him and through the gate. He hazed the cattle down the canyon until he reached the second bend. When he topped a little rise, he could see the three rustlers a half mile ahead.

He drew one of his revolvers, gave a shout, and fired twice in the air. The frightened cattle exploded into a dead run away from him and toward the riders up ahead. One of the rustlers turned in his saddle and looked back to see the oncoming stampede. Buck kept shouting and fired another couple of shots.

The rustlers whipped their ponies and reined to the sides of the canyon to prevent being overrun. Buck ducked low along Patch's neck as he galloped past the surprised men. They fired a few shots in Buck's direction to no effect. In seconds, Buck and the fleeing steers were out of pistol range and charging toward the river. The cattle hit the shallow Nueces and floundered across to the wide floodplain on the west side of the river.

While the cattle were splashing their way across, Buck turned Patch upriver and stopped in a thicket of tall brush. The river had taken the run out of the steers. They stopped and began to scatter while looking back to see if they were still being chased.

The three rustlers forded the river and stopped within a few yards of where Buck hid. "Boys, what do you think that was all about? It looked to me like some Injun was stealin' our herd but where the hell did he go? I know we didn't hit him 'cuz I saw him raise up afore he got to that last little bend. He sure 'nough ain't no Law. Nobody never heard of an Injun lawman. And he can't be workin' for the ranches what owned these beeves 'cuz he wouldn't be here all by his lonesome. I reckon we derned near had our rustled cattle rustled away from us."

Buck stepped out of the brush behind the rustlers with his rifle in one hand and a revolver in the other. He laughed loudly and said, "Some owl hoots you *hombres* make. You let one man steal your stolen herd. And, you best keep your hands up about shoulder high until we get acquainted."

The three men had whirled their ponies around at the first sound of Buck's laugh. They saw that he was well armed and made no sudden moves towards their guns. They kept their hands up as instructed.

One of the men, obviously the group leader, said, "Who in the hell are you and what the dickens are you up to? We ain't no outlaws. Them beeves are ours legal."

"Nobody ever keeps a herd penned up with six different brands on them. If you had them clear and legal, you would have put your own brand on them right away. What is your registered brand, by the way?"

"Bar J," said one of the men.

"Circle dot," said another simultaneously.

"Boys, you'd best get your lies straight," laughed Buck. "It's a good thing I ain't a lawman or working for the ranchers here abouts. If I were, you'd be deader than that rock over yonder. You can put your hands down but don't make any sudden moves. I'd surely hate to shoot fellows that I might want to partner up with. By the by, folks call me Mike. What's your names?"

The leader said, "I'm Joe and that's Sam and Frank. What's your tribe? You don't look Comanche or Kiowa. And, them blue eyes ain't pure Injun."

"I'm part Choctaw from up in the Nations. But that ain't no never mind. You boys had best round up your steers and put 'em back in your brush pen. If I were you, I'd heat me up a D-ring and put a trail brand on them afore some lawman stumbles on them. What are you planning to do with them?"

Joe replied, "We'll gather our herd and brand 'em up like you said. What we plan to do with them ain't really your bidness, but we got a buyer who ranches down in south Texas. He ain't too particular about where the cattle come from since he moves them across the border. And, them Meskins sure don't care where their steers come from. We were told to move whatever we could gather down to the brush country rancho between San Antone and the border.

"I got a little business over on the Frio, but I might catch up with you down south. You plan to skirt Uvalde to the east or to the west?"

"We'll shade to the west far enough that the Marshal in Uvalde don't know we're passin' through. There's too many folks to the east goin' back and forth to San Antone and we don't need to be tanglin' with more folks than we have to."

Buck whistled for Patch to come out of the brush. He swung aboard, tipped his hat, and said, "Don't be surprised if I don't team up with you but I just might. *Adios.*"

XXI

Becky sat at her parents' kitchen table and began a letter to Buck. She had heard nothing from him for weeks. Not a word since the letter saying that he would be on a special mission for the Major.

Is he alive or dead or lying wounded somewhere? I know. I'll write to the Major and ask him about Buck. And, I'll include a letter to Buck for the Major to deliver.

She wrote both letters and then heated the end of a stick of sealing wax over a candle. She sealed both letters and addressed them to Major Jones in care of the Texas Rangers in Austin. After finishing with the letters, she stepped into the parlor where her mother sat mending a torn shirt.

"Momma, may I use the buggy? I've got a couple of letters to post and need to go over to Luke's store to put them in the next batch going out. Do you need anything from the store while I'm there?"

"You writing to Buck again? You shouldn't pin your hopes on that man. Seems to me that he isn't any too anxious to settle down and marry you. You need to fix your plans on one of the young men around here. There are several that are hard working and have good farms. Any one of them would be a good match and provide for you and my grandchildren. That is, if you ever get around to giving me any grandchildren to spoil. And, yes, you can use the buggy. Let me get a list pulled together of what I could use from Luke's store."

Mrs. Griffin put down her sewing and stood. She straightened her apron, bent backwards to take the kinks out of her spine, and walked into the kitchen. After opening several cabinets and the pantry, she said, "I need a spool of white thread and a spool of black, and a few air tights - here let me make a list."

Becky said, "Thanks, Momma. While you are making your list, I'll go and hitch Sandy to the buggy. I'll meet you out front."

★★★

Becky clipped the length of rope on the cast iron tether weight to Sandy's halter. He had a habit of wandering off with the buggy. She climbed the four steps up to the store and walked through the open door. Luke was her dead husband's brother and had inherited the store following the murders of his grandfather and her husband.

"Why, it is a pleasure to see you Sister-In-Law," said a grinning Luke. "What brings you over here on such a fine morning? Have you heard from Buck?"

"Nothing from Buck lately but when he last wrote, he said that he was would be on a special mission and not to expect to hear from him for some time. Here is Momma's list, and I would like to put this in the outgoing mail. How much postage do I owe?"

She paid Luke for the postage and looked through some of the dress material while Luke filled Mrs. Griffin's order. "I just put this on your family's account, okay?" said Luke.

"Yes, Papa will settle up when he next comes in."

Luke loaded Becky's things into the buggy. Gabe Mattingly rode up in a wagon loaded with hay. He looped the reins around the brake arm and climbed down. He tipped his hat to Becky and said, "What a pleasure to see your pretty face. Oh, and howdy to you, Luke."

Luke smiled and said, "I didn't reckon you were talking about my handsome face, were you?"

"Not hardly. I was remarking on this bit of female loveliness," he said as he smiled at Becky. "Ma'am, it would be an honor if you would allow me to help you up into that buggy. And, I would be powerful pleased if you would accompany me to the dance at the meeting hall next week."

"Why, who would have thought that you would turn into a gentleman? I remember how you were always chunking clods at us girls back in school."

"Well, I've wised up considerable since I was ten years old. What about the dance?"

Luke cleared his throat and said, "If you two are going to go to courtin', I'll head back inside. I've got work to do."

Becky laughed and said, "Mr. Mattingly, I will consider your invitation. Stop by the house later in the week, and I'll give you my answer."

While Becky was helping her mother put away the items from the store, she said, "Momma, while I was in the store, Gabe Mattingly pulled up with a wagon load of hay. You remember him from when I was in school, don't you? His family has that farm up the Washita near where we used to catch catfish."

"Yes, I know the family you speak of. Wasn't Gabe that mean little boy that was always throwing things at the other children?"

"Yes, Ma'am, that's him all right. Of course, he has grown up now and I didn't see him throw anything at anyone there at the store. He was very polite, and he asked me to the dance at the meeting hall next week."

"Did you accept?"

"No, I told him I would think about it and that he should stop by here in a few days for my answer."

"Well, why didn't you answer right then? Is he hideous looking or crippled or a drunkard?"

"In fact, he is quite handsome. I saw no sign that he was drinking and did not smell alcohol on him."

"You must have been awful close to him to be able to give him a sniff or two. What were you two up to?"

"Momma, don't be silly. He was a perfect gentleman and helped me up into the buggy."

"If he is that good looking maybe he would make a good husband. Let me know when he is coming for his answer. I will be sure to have a cake or a pie on hand. And for goodness sakes, tell him that you would be happy to have him escort you to the dance. It's not like you are agreeing to marry him. Not yet, anyway!"

XXII

George and his troopers set out due south after filling the water wagon's tank. It took a couple of hours since they had to pass buckets of water from hand to hand up from the river to the water tank.

The surrounding country was dry with scattered patches of brown grasses and a few low growing evergreen bushes, but mostly they crossed coarse sand and gravel. The sun was unrelenting and the ground was blistering hot. With heads down, the men and animals plodded along one weary step at a time. The horizon was flat all around and shimmered in heat waves. The only marks to follow were the tracks of Bill's pony and his flags waving in the hot wind.

As the sun dropped low on the western horizon, Bill appeared ahead of them in the distance. He waved his hat over his head to encourage them on. When they reached him forty minutes later, they were surprised to see a small green valley appear suddenly in front of them.

Bill said, "This country surprises you, don't it? Here is a little river valley that you can't even imagine would be here until you're right on top of it. I think they call this the Huerfano River, though the term 'river' is a bit of a stretch. Anyhow, there's a little water down there. It's gyppy but tolerable. We best water the stock if they'll drink it. My pony drank it and he seems okay. We got three or four days to the Purgatoire River, and it could be dry. We're lucky to have this water. It must have rained some around here in the past few days."

George said, "Thanks for finding it, Bill. Go to the men and have them water the horses and mules. Is there just the one spot with water or is the little river running?"

"No, sir, she ain't runnin' but there's several holes of water up and down this stretch. I'll have the men use the big one for the critters. Then, we can check the other holes to see if any of them are less gyppy."

That night after a dinner of bacon, beans, and coffee, the men scattered around the wagons to lay out their bedrolls and rest a bit before turning in for the night. George checked his duty roster and assigned six of the troopers to take three-hour shifts of watch. Although the threat of Indian attack was small, prudence dictated caution. He let the six men choose with whom they would partner and which shift each pair would take. He had learned that the men obeyed officers that they respected. And, they tended to respect officers who let them share in some of the decisions.

After the first watch had been posted, George gathered his sergeants and scout for a brief meeting. "Men, I calculate that we have come approximately one hundred twenty-five miles since we left Denver. We have nearly seven times that amount of territory yet to cross. Based on the information that Bill and other sources have provided to me, we are about to cross the worst stretch. We have two hundred miles or more from here to the trading post at old Adobe Walls. Some of the country is rough with canyons and steep hills to cross or steer around. There will not be a lot of water to be found, although Bill will do his best to find what there is. Work with your men to show them that we are all in this together. Also, we are likely to encounter a few small Indian raiding parties. Make everyone aware that I would prefer a few false alarms over a lack of vigilance. Also, tell the men that when we reach the trading post at Adobe Walls, the whiskey is on me and we will have a day or two holiday."

They arrived at the canyons of the Purgatoire River in three days. The country was mostly flat and hard packed enough for easy travel except for the scorching sun and limited water. The river had cut a three hundred foot deep canyon that they needed to cross. Bill rode up to George and said, "Lieutenant, it would take days and many miles out of our way to get around this canyon. I've found a place where we can get the wagons across but it will be a bit of work. We will need to ease them down slowly. We can back them down unhitched but restrained by ropes. All of us, and the mules, can work together to get them down. I scouted for a wagon train of pilgrims from St. Joe across to Oregon some years back, and we used this system well. I think it would be best to send the water wagon down first."

"Okay," said George, "show the men what needs to be done. We can't afford to lose our provisions in the supply wagon, so I'll have the men make up some packs and get our food across on mule back. It is late in the day. Let's make camp up here and tackle this problem in the morning. If the men want to climb down to the river to bathe, let them go in groups, but I want at least half of them up here as a precaution against any attack. I know that we have not seen a single human for days, but there is wisdom in caution."

After breakfast the next morning, George asked Bill to explain exactly how the wagon lowering was to be done.

Bill said, "Well, Lieutenant, what we did back on the pilgrim trail was to jack up one of the back wheels on one of the wagons and use that wagon as an anchor and the raised wheel as a windlass. Of course, we blocked the other three wheels good with big rocks. For lowering, we took off the tongue of the wagon to be lowered and tied the end of a stout rope to the tongue-pin hole. Then, we wrapped the rope around the hub of the raised wheel on the anchor wagon. We used that wheel like a windlass to spool off the rope as the other wagon got lowered. Using the brake and a mule team to keep the windlass from spinning, we could control the rate of lowering."

"Ingenious system but I think I can improve it some. I

anticipated that we might encounter the need to pull or lift something heavy during our journey. Let's go to the supply wagon and look at what I included."

George rooted around in the supply wagon and exclaimed, "Aha! Here it is."

"Here's what?" asked Bill.

"A box of pulleys. We can use them to make a block and tackle. That will multiply our force."

The water wagon nearly got away from them, but they got it and the two wagons loaded with the gold, uniforms, and tack down without incident. Only the supply wagon remained since it had served as both anchor and windlass for the other three.

As the men lowered the raised wheel to the ground and removed the stones blocking the other three wheels, George said, "Men, here is what we are going to do. Lash one of the pulleys to that big boulder and the other pulley to the tongue-pin hole in the fifth wheel system. We can run the rope through the two pulleys like so. Now, run the end of the rope back away from the slope and harness it to a team of four mules. Lash the fifth wheel system to keep it straight. Okay, a couple of you push the wagon over to the slope while we back the mule team."

Once the supply wagon reached the bottom of the canyon and all of the men and livestock were down, George called a break for a late lunch.

Bill had ridden upstream a ways and came back with a big smile. He said to George, "Lieutenant, I've found a little side canyon that we can use to get the wagons up to the top. It is not as steep a climb as we had coming down. I think by driving the wagons one at a time using the four-mule and six-mule teams like we did at the Arkansas crossing, we should have no problem. There are one or two rough spots to cross to reach the side canyon, but we'll be fine. We should fill up everything that will hold water before we leave the river."

"That's great news, Bill. Let's get started."

XXIII

Buck rode east up the side canyon and through the rustlers' open brush pen gate. At the far end of the canyon, he dismounted and led Patch up a faint game trail to the top of the first steep hill. He could see that he had crested the divide between the Nueces and Frio watersheds. He only had to work his way down the east side of this hill to enter a valley that would wind its way down to the Frio. Getting down the hill was not going to be easy. The game trail had disappeared and the cedars were especially thick on this slope.

I reckon I'd best tie Patch here and make me a bit of a trail down. Otherwise, I'm liable to have Patch tangle and either run over me or fall on me.

Buck tied Patch's reins to a tree limb and proceeded to break off limbs or hack them off with his Bowie knife. It was hard work and the footing was steep. After three hours, he decided that he had built enough of a trail to get them started. Patch was making a fuss up on the hilltop and was likely to break free and run off.

Buck scrambled back up to where Patch was tied. The horse was thrashing around, neighing, and his ears went laid back. "What the devil's the matter with you, pardner?"

Then, Buck saw the cat. A cougar was crouched forty yards away. The cat's tail was twitching back and forth as he prepared to attack the horse. Buck jerked his revolver and fired two shots just to the left of the cougar. The cat bolted and disappeared over the west side of the hill. Patch began to settle down.

"I know, I know, you wanted me to kill him but he wasn't going to be a threat with me here. Of course, those owl hoots down the west side may lose a steer if they don't be mindful. Come on, let's get down off of this hill."

Buck led Patch down the crude trail he had built until the slope became less steep. They did slip and slide a bit, but Patch managed to keep his feet under him and Buck managed to scamper out of the horse's way. They stopped to take a breather before Buck swung back into the saddle. "I think we can bust our way through the last of these cedars and get down yonder to that dry creek bed, Ol' Hoss. Let's do it."

They crashed their way to the bottom of the slope. Although Buck's face was bleeding in several spots where branches had lashed him, the wounds were minor. He dismounted to wipe his face and check Patch over to be certain that the horse had not sustained any significant injuries. Once certain that Patch was okay, he remounted and proceeded down the dry creek bed to the floodplain of the Frio.

Buck tied Patch to a hitching rail outside a small sawmill. Three men were working to saw planks from huge cypress logs. Buck waited for them to take a break, which would decrease the noise of the saw sufficiently to allow for conversation.

The oldest of the three men looked up and spotted Buck. He jumped to where he had propped a rifle, grabbed it, and shouted, "Injuns!" The two young men jumped back from their work and whirled to face Buck.

Buck raised both hands to shoulder level and said, "Peace, I am no threat to you, and I am only part Indian. I am looking for a Mr. Watkins. Sir, are you Mr. Watkins?"

The older man lowered his rifle a bit and said, "No, my name is John Leakey. Your red skinned brethren have been up to mischief around here lately. And, we'd just as soon have your kind stay out of our valley. The Watkins outfit is six or seven miles south at Rio Frio. What do you want from him?"

"I hear that he has some Bois D'Arc trees. I have need of a bit of Bois D'Arc wood. You don't have any that you would sell, do you?"

"Nope, I got no use from them trees, and folks around here don't cotton to them big horse apples litterin' the ground. The young'uns have a habit of chunkin' them at folks and them damn things can knock a feller out."

"I'll let you men get back to your work and be on my way."

Buck backed away, turned toward the hitching rail, and untied Patch. He mounted and rode south at a lope until he felt he was safely out of rifle range. *I'll need to get a message to the Major that these folks seem to still be having trouble with Indian raids. They looked like they would just as soon shoot me as give me information. Maybe a scout through here by a few Rangers would calm things down a bit? When I get down to Rio Frio, I best be on my guard and make it clear that I am peaceable.*

Two hours later, Buck splashed across the shallow river and rode toward the little village. He spotted the stand of Bois D'Arc trees halfway between the river and the town. He turned Patch in that direction. Prosperous looking farms were all around. A network of irrigation ditches brought river water to the fields.

At what had to be the Watkins farm, Buck called out, "Hello, the house, I am looking for Mr. Watkins."

A man called out from the barn situated one hundred yards to the right of the house. "I'm Watkins. Who are you?"

Buck unfastened his gun belt and held it over his head as he walked Patch to the barn. He dismounted and removed his badge from the pocket on the gun belt as he draped the belt and revolver over his saddle horn. He walked toward Mr. Watkins holding the badge in front of him.

Once he determined that they were alone, he said, "Mr. Watkins, I am Caleb McDougal of the Texas Rangers. I am in this disguise on a special and secret mission to determine who is behind cattle rustling and other crimes in this area of the state. The State of Texas needs for you to keep my identity secret. Can you agree to that?"

"Well, of course, but you are going to get yourself shot parading around looking like an Indian. Too many families in this part of the state have come to grief over the raids."

"Thanks for your concern, but my disguise is necessary to my mission."

"Why did you come looking for me?"

"I need a limb or two from one of your Bois D'Arc trees. You see I am part Indian. My mother was Choctaw back in Tennessee. She taught my brothers and me to make a strong bow from the wood of trees like yours. Some of the cattle thieves and murderers have been disguising their crimes so as to make folks think they had been victims of Indians. I have been fighting Comanches and Kiowas off and on for over a year and certainly have no love for them. But criminals, red or brown or white, are a problem for all law-abiding folks. The Rangers plan to clean all of them up."

"Of course you can have whatever you need from my trees. You are welcome to grain your horse and rest here for a day or two if you like, but I would be careful about riding over there into town. We had two families murdered by Indians a year or so back and folks have strong feelings yet."

"I'll take you up on your offer, but I'll sleep in your barn so as to put you and your family to no extra trouble. Please tell your family nothing about my true identity. Perhaps you could explain my presence as a half-breed Indian seeking revenge against Comanche raiders. Also, is there a post office in town?"

"Yes, we have a post office."

"Here is money to cover postage. I need to write a couple of letters. Could you take them to the post office for me?"

"Of course, that will be no problem. We generally make a trip to town on Saturday so the Missus can do some shopping. That's the day after tomorrow. I'll gladly take your letters."

★★★

Buck pulled a few small scraps of paper, a little stick of sealing wax, and a stub of a pencil from his saddlebag. He sat on a couple of feed sacks in one of the stalls of the barn and wrote, in code, a brief report to Major Jones and outlined his plans for the near future. He addressed the letter to Jacob Jones in care of General Delivery Kerrville, Texas. The second letter was to Becky.

That finished, he walked out of the barn carrying a saw that he borrowed from the farm tool shed. He selected a straight limb for the bow and cut it from the tree. Then from a thicket of red oaks, he trimmed a dozen shoots, which he would use to make arrows. He carried it all back to the barn and carefully began shaping the bow. He built a typical hunting bow of about three and one-half feet in length. Since he used a green limb for the bow there was a possibility that it would split once dry or during use, so he wrapped it with wet sinew. Then, once it had dried, he added a very thin coat of hide glue.

He did not want to overstay his welcome at the Watkins farm, so the next morning, he thanked Mr. Watkins and bid him goodbye. He rode south for a couple of hours before crossing the river and making an early camp in a cedar thicket on the west side of the canyon.

He shaped his arrows by drawing the branches through a round hole he had made in a deer scapula. He fletched his arrows with hide glue and turkey feathers and added the iron points that Angry had given him. *Not perfect, but it'll do,* he thought. He then used a deer hide to fashion a quiver for his arrows.

San Saba Gold

XXIV

Bob Clarke sat on his horse at the meeting site in the brush country south of the little village of Carrizo Springs. He was in the middle of a huge ranch that bordered the Rio Grande on the south and spread over five hundred sections, close to a third of a million acres. His men were holding a herd of five hundred rustled cattle that they had gathered to deliver to the Boss. Bob had always met the Boss at night and never closer to the man than twenty feet. He did not know his name nor did he care. In fact, he did not really know what the man looked like. If that was the way the Boss wanted to do business, it suited Bob just fine. The Boss paid good money and asked no questions as to the source of the cattle that Bob and his men delivered.

Bob liked his new arrangement. The days of stealing a few head for hides up on the Llano and scaring the locals into thinking that Indians had done it were long past.

Suddenly a match flared in the darkness as a rider rode into the clearing. The glow of his cigar identified the rider to Bob as the Boss.

Bob said, "Boss, we've got a herd of five hundred steers bedded down about a mile west. Do you want us to drive them on down to the crossing into Mexico like last time?"

"Yes, Don Mendoza's men will meet you as before. Meet me back here in one week and you will receive your money."

"Yes, sir, *hasta luego.*"

Buck stayed where he was hidden until the rustler and

Boss rode their separate ways. He had hobbled Patch and left him to graze a half mile north in a little pocket of grass surrounded by a seven-foot tall wall of brush. The south Texas brush country is a huge expanse of tall, dense, thorny brush that stretches over a vast area from San Antonio to the Rio Grande on the west and south and to the coastal plain on the east. In many areas, it is virtually impenetrable. Huge rattlesnakes abound as do virtually every other animal known to Texas and northern Mexico.

Buck quietly eased his way back to where he had left Patch. He saddled the horse and removed the hobbles. As he swung aboard, he thought, *I sure wish I had some of those thick leather chaparejos that the Mexican vaqueros wear. These stickers are something fierce. My legs are scratched from the top of my moccasins to my knees, and my arms and face are pretty chewed up as well. But, I reckon that chaparejos wouldn't fit to well with my Indian garb.*

The breeze shifted around to the southwest and Buck could soon smell the distinctive aroma and hear the bawling of cattle. *That must be the rustlers' herd yonder way. I'll ease around to the south and see if I can get to where I can see them as they drive the herd toward the border.*

A very wet Buck sat astride Patch in the early dawn light as he tried to peer through the dense fog that had settled over the countryside. Cardinals, the early risers of the bird world, began announcing the day from several directions. Tom turkeys gobbled in the brush and coyotes set up their last serenade of the night. The rising sun quickly burned off the fog layer and gave promise to the scorching heat of the day.

The rustlers were up early, too. Buck could hear the cattle bawling as they were being pushed south. A fairly wide trail, more or less north to south, lay just to the west of him. He doubted that it was a natural trail through the brush. It was too straight for one thing. Nature was not known for creating many trails that were straight.

As the herd passed abreast of him, Buck stood in his

stirrups to peer over the tops of the brush around him. One of the men on the near flank sat his horse in a familiar way. Buck realized the man was Sam, one of the rustlers he had met in the Nueces River canyon.

It appears that small time thieves all over this region know about this 'Boss' fellow and his arrangements with the Mexican, Don Mendoza. I'll ease over to Sam and see if I can join into this crowd.

Buck gigged Patch with his heels and worked his way through the brush until he was at the edge of the wide trail. He pulled out alongside Sam.

"Why, hello, Sam, remember me? I'm Mike. I had a little fun with you boys and your steers up on the Nueces."

Startled, Sam jerked up wide-awake. He had been dozing. "Lordy, you give me a fright poppin' outta the bresh like that. Yeah, I remember you, and your little sport warn't no fun fer us. It took all day to get them steers back into that bresh trap. What in hell you doin' here?"

"I told you boys that I'd try to catch up with you but I was delayed over in the Rio Frio country. I followed your trail down to here."

"What's with the bow and quiver of arrers? You gone full Injun?"

"Sam, there's times when I need to kill something without making a whole lot of racket. Besides, if I need to shoot somebody, the law will blame it on the Lipans or the Kickapoos. No sense having them looking for me."

Bob Clarke rode out front on point with two other men. As was his practice, he would occasionally ride around the herd to ensure that all was going according to plan. He swung his pony around to the right so that he could work back along the west side of the herd. He turned away as he neared the drags at the rear of the herd. He would sit a bit to let most of the dust settle before swinging around to the east side of the herd.

Due to the narrowness of the trail, the cattle were spread in a line a half-mile long. As Bob looked across to the east side, he could see the young cowboy riding drag on that side and the man riding the left rear flank position. He pulled his bandana up to cover his nose and mouth so as to limit the amount of dust he would breathe. He eased east through the thinning brown dust and then south until he was a quarter mile behind the left rear flank drover but out of the drags. He gave a cluck and gigged his heels into his pony's flanks to come up to a trot.

As he neared the drover he said, "Ever'thin' okay, Chet?"

"Yepper, Mr. Clarke, these beeves is good and trail broke. I only had to push one or two out of the bresh and back into the herd. But there's something a mite queer up yonder," he said as he pointed toward the head of the herd.

"What do you mean queer?"

"Well, sir, a little while ago a Injun popped outta the bresh and he's ridin' along with Sam like they's *compadres*. Looka yonder, he's got a bow over his back and he's dressed all in buckskins. He's a redskin fer sure. What you reckon that's all about?"

"Hell if I know, but I damn sure mean to find out," said Bob as he spurred his pony to a canter.

Bob reined to a halt just behind Sam and Buck. He drew his revolver and said, "Who in the hell are you? Are you okay, Sam?"

"I'm fine, Bob. This here's a half-breed feller what calls hisself Mike. We run into him up in the Nueces country. He played sorta a trick on us and seems like he's okay. If'n you know what I mean?"

Buck turned his pony back to pull along side Bob's horse and said, "I'm sorta in the same line of work as you fellers, but I've done most of my loose rope work up in the Nations. The law and the Cherokees up that-a-way got a little too interested in me so's I've been driftin' down into this country to see if I could hire on to a group of like-minded cattlemen. Can you use another hand?"

"Appears to me that you're just ridin' the chuck line. I don't need another hand for this drive, but I'll make you a proposition. You ride nighthawk and I'll feed you. No pay. If you work out, we can see about the next drive."

Buck knew that he was being tested. No self-respecting waddie would accept such terms unless he was truly desperate. "Well, that's a mighty generous offer, but I reckon I'll just strike out on my own for a bit. There seem to be a lot of lightly tended steers just north of here. Maybeso I'll throw together a little herd of my own. If Sam and the two yahoos he rides with can manage to make a gather without getting caught, I won't have no problem. Hell, I ran off with their herd easy as pie up on the Nueces. If'n I'd been serious, I would have kept them. *Adios.*"

Buck tipped his hat, gave a wave, and disappeared back into the brush. Bob turned to Sam and said, "That feller a friend of yours?"

"No, siree! I jist said I knowed who he was. Up yonder on the Nueces, he run our little herd out of a bresh trap and then let us have 'em back. I reckon he's jist sorta a maverick and maybe a little *loco.*"

San Saba Gold

XXV

It took the remainder of the day to get the wagons and livestock up to the top of the Purgatoire River canyon, but they managed without incident. While George and the troopers struggled to get everything up the slope, Bill loped off to scout a route for them.

Bill rode into camp just as the men were eating their supper. He handed the reins of his horse to a soldier who was the stock wrangler of the expedition. He spooned beans onto a tin plate and poured himself a cup of coffee. He walked over to where George was sitting and sat cross-legged on the hard ground.

"Lieutenant, we have an easy route tomorrow of about fifteen miles or so heading south by southeast. After that we need to head east by northeast for two and a half or three days to get around a whole mess of rough country where the Cimarron River has cut up the land for miles. That'll put us a day or so north of a skinny stretch called the Neutral Strip that used to be part of Texas back before the War but is now a 'No Man's Land'. My guess is that there's either nobody there or it's full of Injuns and outlaws like much of the Injun Nations. It'll take two good days to get across it and into Texas, and pritnear another week to the Adobe Walls."

"Well, Bill, if that's the route you pick then we'll get to it first thing in the morning."

It took a hard dry week to reach the crossing of the Cimarron deep inside the Neutral Strip. The men and animals were thirsty because there was little water left. What they had, they gave to the livestock. The water in the Cimarron was too salty and gyppy to drink.

Bill said, "Lieutenant, Flagg Spring is only twelve or fifteen miles south. It sits along the old Santa Fe Trail and the water is good. Plus, there's plenty of it."

George said, "Okay, Bill, gather the men."

Once the men had circled where George stood on one of the wagon seats, he said, "Men, the river water is no good and will just make us sick. Keep the horses and mules away from the river. We don't want them sick. They smell the water, so if we stay here, we will need to picket them between two of the wagons.

"Bill says there's plenty of good water at a spring south of here. Instead of waiting until morning, I propose that we have a quick cold supper and head out now. We will have plenty of moonlight tonight and we can get there before daybreak. Anybody against pressing on? Okay, the mules are tired so we'll use our horses to pull the wagons and we will all walk except for the drivers. We can switch drivers every so often to give our legs a rest. We'll switch out the horses every two or three hours. Bill will lead out a-horseback to mark our trail. Let's get to it."

At the spring, Bill and the wrangler watered the horses and mules while the men stripped off their uniforms and soaked in the reviving water. George stood in waist deep water and wrung out his clothing that he had rinsed of dust and sweat. He said, "Men, when you finish your swimming party, wash out your uniforms. We have a bit more than a week to reach whatever is left of the old Adobe Walls trading post and aren't likely to find this much fresh water until we get there. Two of you go relieve Bill and Private Faulstich with the stock watering. Let them have a chance to soak."

After everyone had rehydrated a bit, the cooks started preparing supper while the rest of the men set up a more orderly camp. As the men lined up to fill their plates, George announced, "Men, I have decided that we will remain here tomorrow to give you and the animals a chance to rest. Bill and I will ride out a ways to select a route and scout for signs of outlaws or Indians. Enjoy your supper and get some rest. We will use just two guards at a time in four-hour shifts. You men know whose turn it is for night watch."

Spotted Fox and Big Tooth were thirteen-year-old Kiowa boys. They had tired of the tales of bravery told around the fires by the men and older boys of the camp. Now that the whites had kept the tribe penned on the reservation, there was little opportunity for youngsters like themselves to show that they too deserved warrior status.

One night they quietly led their ponies away from the camp. Once well clear of the camp, they mounted and rode northwest beyond the boundaries of the reservation. Twice the soldiers in the hats had nearly spotted them but they had been lucky. Twelve sleeps later they were chasing a small herd of buffalo when they stumbled into a large prairie dog town. Both ponies stumbled and fell with broken legs.

They were lost and afoot two hundred and fifty miles from their families. That night they cooked a bit of meat from one of their ponies and sat sadly without looking at each other. Finally, Big Tooth said, "What are we to do? I do not want to be ridiculed by the men if we come walking into camp without our ponies and nothing to show for our travels."

Spotted Fox replied, "I think we should keep going northwest. The old ones tell of great mountains in that direction and many horses in the towns of the whites. We can carry plenty of meat from our dead ponies, and we have come a very long way. Surely the mountains cannot be much farther. I do not want to return without horses and maybe even some scalps. We should cook as much of this meat as we can carry and then rest. I am tired."

At first light, the boys ate, packed up whatever they

could carry, and plodded off across the dry, desolate land. At midday, they stopped to rest and ate a little of the roasted horseflesh. "I smell wood smoke," said Big Tooth.

"I smell it now also. The wind blows from the west. Let's go see where it comes from. Perhaps it is a camp of some of our people who did not move to the reservation. Many of the old men tell of bands who did not surrender to the whites."

The boys hurried to the west but dropped to the ground just before they crested a small rise. Spotted Fox said, "We should be careful. It could be pony soldiers or other whites. Let's crawl to the top and see what is beyond this hill."

They belly crawled through the tall grass to the top of the little hill. Below them was a shallow river canyon that stretched off into the distance. Camped on the near side of the canyon was a troop of pony soldiers with four wagons. One of the wagons was odd looking with a very large wooden barrel on it. Most important to the boys was a small herd of horses and mules. If they could steal horses from the pony soldiers, they could ride proudly into their home camp. All would see that they were brave and worthy of admiration.

Spotted Fox tapped his companion on the shoulder and slithered backward down the grassy slope until he was certain that none of the soldiers would see him when he stood. He and Big Tooth ran quickly to where they had left their packs.

Spotted Fox said, "We must go back to that buffalo wallow where we camped last night. Tonight we will return and steal some ponies from those soldiers. Then we can ride back to the reservation as men."

The boys dozed fitfully in the shallow depression. Big Tooth awoke and walked out of the wallow to relieve his bladder. He stared up into a sky filled with stars. The moon hung low in the western sky. He judged the night to be more than half over as he hastened back to where Spotted Fox slept. He shook his friend's shoulder and softly said, "I think it is time for us to steal some ponies."

They crept back to the small hill and satisfied themselves that the soldiers' horses remained in the same area where they had seen them in the late afternoon. Two soldiers were standing guard between the horses and the soldier camp.

Spotted Fox said, "They are foolish. The guards should be on the side of the ponies away from the camp. The campfire that they are looking towards will blind them to the dark. Let's move around to the far side of the pony herd. The wind is bad for us because it comes from the side where we must go, but I have an idea. Here rub yourself all over with this green grass and sage brush so that the ponies do not smell us as a threat."

The boys slowly crept up to the horse herd. Big Tooth used his knife to cut the rope the soldiers had tied between two trees to form a makeshift picket line. He coiled it up and hung it over his right shoulder. The boys had kept their plaited rawhide bridles tied around their waists. They slipped these off and eased up to the two nearest horses. They held fresh green grass up to the horses' muzzles and slipped the rawhide bit into the interdental space of the animals' lower jaws. A third horse standing next to the other two wore a halter left on by one of the soldiers. Spotted Fox took the coil of rope from Big Tooth and tied it to the third horse's halter. They swung aboard and jabbed their heels into their horses' ribs and were off at a gallop. The third horse balked a bit and Spotted Fox felt the lead rope tighten. The horse fought the rope a bit and snorted. The snort brought the guards to full alert. They immediately fired at the fleeing boys.

Spotted Fox was nearly unseated when the big .45 caliber slug slammed into his back. The bullet entered just above his right shoulder blade and exited from his chest just below his collarbone. Blood was pouring from both wounds. Big Tooth looked back and shouted, "Are you hit?"

Spotted Fox could only moan in reply. He had dropped the lead rope to the third horse and was losing consciousness. Big Tooth slowed until he was along side his friend. He held

Spotted Fox on his horse as best he could, but this meant that they would have to ride slowly. Surely the soldiers would be coming.

An hour past midnight, George was awakened by the sound of rifle shots and shouts from the men on guard duty. The entire camp was on their feet and scrambled for weapons in just seconds. One of the guards, Corporal Morris, ran to George and said, "Indians, Sir, two of them sneaked in on foot. They made off with three of our horses before I could get a shot off. But as they rode away, I think I hit one of them."

George shouted, "Bill, take six men and get after them. We need those horses."

Bill said, "Yes, Sir, but it'll be tough tracking them in the dark. If they come up from the Nations, I expect they'll make a run for the reservation southeast of here, but that's a long way off and they could-a been Apaches coming from the south or southwest. We'll do our best."

Bill rode out a quarter mile ahead of the troopers and dismounted. He led his horse in a big arc to the southeast and soon found a trail where the grass was just springing back up. He followed only a few yards before he bent down to look in the dark at what appeared to be a blackish liquid on the grass. As he brought his fingers up near his face he realized that it was red not black. *Blood, Morris did hit one of them or one of the horses,* he thought. He swung back into the saddle and whistled for the troopers to join him.

"Men, they're headed for the Nations and leaving a blood trail. Let's form a line and head southeast. See how the grass is bent down where they passed? Keep an eye out for it and sing out if you see a change in their direction. We should be able to catch them if we hurry. One of them is bleeding."

A quarter mile further, Corporal Morris shouted, "Look yonder, there's one of our horses."

As they rode up, the horse tried to shy away but its feet were entangled in the lead rope that Spotted Fox had tied to the halter. Bill dismounted, untangled the rope, and checked the horse for wounds. Finding none, he said, "Corporal Morris' shot must have hit one of the Indians. They can't travel fast with a wounded man. I need one of you to volunteer to take this horse back to camp. The rest of us need to light out after the thieves."

One of the privates volunteered to return the short distance back to camp. He asked Bill, "Should I come back and trail you once I return the horse?"

"No, there are enough of us to deal with two Indians. One of them is hurt and maybe dying. Look at how much blood we have seen so far."

Spotted Fox said weakly, "Stop, my brother, I can go no farther. I feel that I am slipping away to join the Spirit World. Leave me here and ride hard to escape. Take this pony with you so that you can tell the elders that I died bravely."

"I will not leave you here to be desecrated by the pony soldiers. I will wait with you until your Spirit leaves. Then, I will find a secret place to bury your body."

Spotted Fox moaned once more and slipped from the horse's back. Big Tooth held his friend until the last breath rattled from him. Then he laid Spotted Fox's lifeless body across the back of the horse. He took off his own leggings and used his knife to split them lengthwise so that the resulting buckskin was long enough to tie Spotted Fox to the horse. He remounted his own horse and led Spotted Fox's horse behind him as he rode across the rolling prairie.

Big Tooth knew that he should be moving faster but he feared that Spotted Fox's body would fall from the horse if they proceeded faster than a steady lope. As the sky began to lighten in the east, he saw a tree line off to his right. He decided to hide there until the soldiers passed. He was certain that they were coming.

The tree line followed a little dry creek bed. Big Tooth soon found an overhang where he could place Spotted Fox's body. Using his knife, he quickly weakened the underside of the overhanging clay bank sufficiently to cave in the soil to bury his friend. That done, he led the two horses away from the grave and hid in the gully formed by the little creek.

His wait was short, no more than an hour. The soldiers were coming toward the place where he had first entered the creek bed. The man in front leaned over his saddle and studied the ground. He was obviously a good tracker. Five pony soldiers followed behind the tracker. Big Tooth wished he had an older man to tell him whether he should try to run or stay hidden. He had always relied on Spotted Fox to make most of their decisions. He had his bow and knew he could kill one or two of the soldiers before they killed him, but he felt certain that he could not escape. Maybe they would not find him and they would leave?

Bill reined up at the lip of the creek bed and said, "Men, they entered this little gully here. I don't see any sign that they climbed out on the other side, at least not here. Three of you ease down the gully to the west. The other two follow me to the east. Go slow and look for tracks but keep an eye out for an ambush. There's two of them and one of them isn't hurt. They'll stick you full of arrows if you get careless."

Bill had not gone more than forty yards before he spotted the hoof prints in a stretch of sand. "Corporal Morris, go get those three men who went west, our Indians left these tracks and are up ahead somewhere."

Bill and the trooper waited until the other three joined them. Bill said, "Here's my idea. You fellers split up and ride along the top on either side of the creek. I'll ease along in the creek bed and see if I can flush them out. Keep your weapons at the ready 'cuz they're liable to bust out at a run. If'n they decide to stick and fight, we'll have them boxed."

XXVI

Luke looked up from a column of figures in the ledger he had on the counter in front of him. He smiled broadly and said, "Why, how are you today, Miss Becky?"

"I'm fine, Luke. I've got a little list of things for Momma."

"I'll fill it right away. And, there's a letter here for you. It looks like Buck's handwriting," he said with a big grin. "Do you want the letter?"

"Luke, don't be teasing. Of course, I want the letter."

"Well, I know you went to that dance with Gabe Mattingly and have been seen out riding in a buggy with him. I sorta figured that you had cooled towards Ol' Buck and found yourself a new steady beau."

"Gabe is just a good friend. I still have feelings for Buck and will wait for him a bit longer."

"Well, I've seen the way that Gabe looks at you and pritnear goes plumb foolish when you are around. I reckon that Gabe has more than just friendship in mind."

"Just fill Momma's order and hand me the letter. I'll be sitting on the bench out front. Holler when you have the order ready."

Becky carefully opened the crudely sealed letter and unfolded the rough brown paper. *I bet he made that sorry looking gob of sealing wax himself. Looks about like something a man would make. And, this paper looks like something a store wrapped bacon in. It's got grease spots all over it. At least, he managed this time to write more than 'Hi, I'm fine',* she thought. Buck's letter began,

Dearest Becky,

I hope you haven't forgotten me. I think of you every day. I'm down in south Texas working on the job I mentioned in my previous letter. The weather is exceedingly warm and my horse, Patch, and I are in good health. The place where I sit is in a beautiful valley with a clear fast flowing river.

The people here are friendly, though they were initially hostile since I appear Indian to them. I have let my hair grow long and wear buckskins. And, of course, I ride a Comanche Medicine Hat paint horse. I explained to them my reason for the appearance and they have taken my word for it.

You can tell Luke and your father that I have made a bow and some arrows in the old way. I am pretty accurate with it though I am not much good at long distances. My mother was a very good archer and I am nowhere near as proficient as she was.

I hope to finish my assignment in no more than two months. When this work is done, I will resign and return to you for good if you'll have me.

Buck

Becky folded the letter back into the crude shape Buck had used and stuck it in the pocket of her apron. Just then, Luke stepped out onto the gallery that ran along the front of the store. "Your order is ready," he said. "Look, yonder comes Gabe. I'll bet a Yankee dollar that he will be glad to see you here."

"Oh hush, don't you go to egging him on or stirring up anything. Remember I just want Gabe as a friend."

Gabe's team and wagon rumbled up dragging a huge

cloud of red dust. "Oh, Miss Becky, I'm powerful sorry to raise this dust on you. I didn't see you sitting there or I'd have stopped back a-ways."

"Gabe Mattingly, if red dust were to kill a body, everybody in the territory would have all choked to death years ago. I'm just here for a minute to pick up some things that Momma needs right away. Soon as Luke loads them into the buggy, I've got to scamper back home."

"Now, Becky, surely you can spare a few minutes to talk with me?"

"Okay, but only for a minute or two."

Luke smirked to himself as he slowly finished loading Becky's buggy. He began to whistle a lively ditty as he sauntered back into the store.

Gabe climbed down from his wagon and walked over to where Becky stood. He said, "You know that we have had some fun together and we are friends, aren't we?"

"Yes, we are friends," Becky tried to emphasize the last word.

"Well, I would like for us to become more than just friends. I would like to speak to your father about me courting you properly."

Becky had feared that this was coming. She blurted, "Well, Gabe, you see I am already spoken for."

Had she read more in Buck's letter than he intended? Or, was the closing of his letter a clumsy proposal? *Lordy, why does everything have to get so complicated?*

"Spoken for? Who? When? I thought you were still in mourning. Or, at least a little bit in mourning."

"Gabe, you may not remember that I was courted by Buck McDougal for a while before I married James. And, surely you have heard the story of how Buck rescued me from those Mexicans. Well, Buck has asked me to wait for him to return and I intend to wait."

"Buck? Buck? Hel…heck, he ain't been around here more than a few days in the last year. I heard that he joined the Texas Rangers, and most folks figure that he'll either get himself killed or become a permanent Texican. And, he ain't even full Choctaw."

"Well, Gabe, that's the straight of it. I still value your friendship. But, that's all it can be. I am sorry if I gave you a wrong impression. Now, I have to leave as Momma is waiting for these things from the store. Goodbye."

Becky climbed aboard the buggy, clucked a couple of times, and gave the reins a little slap across the horse's rumps. Gabe stood there with his mouth agape staring after her through the red dust kicked up by the buggy.

Luke poked his head out of the door and said with a laugh, "You're likely to catch a fly or two if you don't close your mouth."

"You mind your own business, storekeep. I've got better things to be doing than to listen to the likes of you."

XXVII

Buck sat in the sparse shade of a crudely built brush arbor next to a shabby adobe building. His command of the Spanish language was meager. The best he was able to determine from the Mexican inside the building was that this place was called *Javelina*. It wasn't up to what one would call a town or even a village. In addition to the adobe building, which served as a sort of store and cantina, six or seven rough *jacals* were haphazardly scattered about. A few dusty, stinking goat pens had been hacked into the surrounding brush and cactus.

Buck was filthy. He had not had access to enough clean water to bathe in a couple of weeks. His buckskins were in deplorable condition. The pants were stained nearly black from his sweat, bacon grease from his cooking, and the sweat of his horse. Most of the decorative fringes and beadwork so carefully done by the Shoshone woman were gone. His sleeves were patched, as was the seat of his pants. *I reckon I'm a sorry sight and a bit fragrant, too. No wonder that barkeeper inside the cantina gave me a look of disgust.*

Buck had entered the cantina and asked for fresh water. The proprietor had responded *no agua dulce aqui solamente pulque*, which he decided that the man meant no sweet water here and something about that milky alcoholic beverage the poor Mexicans drank. He thanked the man and walked out the door looking for a water well. *Surely these folks have got to have water and there ain't no creek handy. And, by the by, where are the people? Seems to be nobody here except that surly barkeeper.*

He sat there on the bench with his head bowed as through he were napping. In reality, he was watching from under the shadow of his wide brimmed hat. After twenty minutes, he detected a bit of movement in one of the *jacals.* Then he saw the head of a small boy peeking around the corner of the cantina.

"*Muchacho viene aqui, por favor,*" said Buck hoping that he got that right in Spanish.

The boy stepped out in the open and ventured a hesitant step or two toward where Buck sat. "*Donde esta el agua,*" Buck said as he mimicked drinking from a cup.

The boy pointed toward the backside of the cantina before giggling and running into the nearest *jacal.*

Buck stood and walked slowly around the far side of the cantina and looked in the direction the boy had pointed. Four large wooden barrels sat upright on rough-hewn mesquite logs along the back wall of the cantina. Over them was a makeshift arbor of limbs supported by cedar posts and covered by a woven mat of yucca leaves. The arbor provided a bare modicum of shade to the barrels. Beside them sat a big-wheeled Mexican cart.

Buck eased up the wooden lid of one of the barrels and jumped back as a leopard frog sprung out and hopped away. The water inside was fairly clear but a dark rusty brown in color. He turned the bung tap at the bottom of the barrel and a stream of the brown water ran out. He shut off the tap and tried the other three barrels. One was empty but the other two provided similar water. He chose the one that did not appear to have any wildlife swimming or hopping in it and took a little taste. It had a swampy taste. He spit it out. *Well, that's about as good as I'm likely to find. I reckon that was frog I tasted.* He washed some of the grime from his face and walked back to the front of the cantina.

Buck stepped into the dark, low ceilinged room and moved sideways away from the door. Experience had taught him that he made less of a target if he was not backlit when entering a dark room. As his eyes adjusted to the dim light, he saw that he was alone except for the proprietor.

"*Señor, mi Español es muy malo. Usted habla ingles?*"

"*Si,* I speak your language. What do you want now? More water? I heard you out back. Water is scarce here and must be hauled by wagon from a well on the *rancho* of *Señor* Hartright. We must pay him for that water. I will only charge you one gringo dollar for what you used."

"I'll tell you what. I'll pay you that dollar whenever you have some clear, clean water. I've drunk out of horse troughs that were better than that. If you really pay this Hartright *hombre* for that water, you should be outside digging your own well. And, where are all the folks that live in the shacks outside? I've only seen one small boy."

"The people are hiding. Many *pistoleros*, like yourself, come through here and abuse the women and sometimes shoot the men. At the very least, they kill a kid goat or two for *cabrito* and they do not pay the owner."

"Well, I mean these folks no harm, and I won't steal their goats or abuse their women. What is your name? I am called Mike. Who is the best cook in the village?"

"My name is Hector Santiago. *Señora* Martinez cooks better than most, but these people are very poor and have little to eat."

"Call for her. Does she speak English?"

"No, only I speak a little *ingles aqui*."

"I'll pay you that dollar if you call her here and translate for me."

"Okay, I will call her and see if she will talk with you."

Buck went back to the brush arbor next to the cantina and sat on the crude bench. After twenty minutes or so, Hector shuffled out of the surrounding brush. Walking beside him was a stooped, elderly Mexican woman. She gave Buck a fearful look and pulled back from Hector.

Buck stood and said, "*Señora,* I mean you no harm. I would like to pay you to cook a meal for me and perhaps for all of your people."

Hector translated and then said to Buck, "There is very little food here. Of course, there are the goats and their milk, some *frijoles*, and masa for tortillas but little else and no excess for visitors."

Buck said, "I've got a hankering for beef. What say, I bring in a steer and we butcher it? You can have some of the men dig us a bit of a fire pit where we can cook it. *Señora* Martinez can get some of the women to help her cook up a pot of beans and whatever to go with the beef."

"But, there are no cattle in the village and the gringo ranchers will not allow us to take one of theirs."

"Leave that to me," said Buck. "No one will bother your people about the steer I bring."

Buck rode out of the brush and up to the front of the cantina. He dismounted and stepped inside. No one was there but he could hear voices out back. Around back, he found four men building a fire pit at Hector's direction.

Buck said, "What you got to pull that cart? I shot a couple of steers out in the brush and we need to haul them over here to skin 'em and cut up the meat. I've already gutted and split them. I used my horse to hoist them up into a couple of mesquites so that the ants won't get them, but the other varmints will be at them pronto if we don't haul them back right away."

Hector spoke to a couple of the men and they ran off into the brush. A few minutes later, they returned with two good-sized burros and began harnessing them to the cart.

Hector said, "*Señor* Mike, Carlos will follow you with the cart. Two of the young men will come to help with the loading. But do not get caught. Your shots came from the direction of *Señor* Hartright's land. If he or his *vaqueros* catch you, they will kill you without asking questions."

"I will watch but I can handle whatever comes up."

Buck remounted Patch and led the Mexicans down the dusty road to the south. In less than an hour, they were back at the cantina with the cart and dead steers.

"Hector, let's get these beeves skinned out and the meat cut up and on the fire."

A large crowd of Mexicans had arrived, more than lived in the *jacals* of *Javelina*. Word had spread fast in the surrounding brush country that there was to be a bit of a *fiesta*. After dark, the fire pit and a great many *luminarias* provided ample light for the people to dance as a few of the talented ones strummed guitars and sawed away at fiddles. One young man who had a good voice sang and another played a concertina. Buck sat on a blanket at the edge of the clearing as did many of the men who were not dancing with the women and girls. Hector, who was quite drunk on *pulque*, sat next to Buck.

Hector said, "*Señor,* we must bury those hides or there will be much trouble. They bear the 'J-H' brand of *Señor* Hartright. He will be very angry if he finds that we are eating his cattle."

"I will keep the hides," said Buck. "I have a use for them. Also, can you tell me why there is a wide strip of cleared brush running north and south through the Hartright ranch?"

"Ay yi yi, it is best not to talk of such things. A man could get killed discussing what goes on around here. Let us just say that from time to time one can hear a great many cattle moving south through the brush, often at night when the moon is full."

"Do you know if Mr. Hartright knows of these movements?"

"*Quien sabe*, the *rancho* is quite large. The *hacienda* is miles away to the east and *Señor* Hartright is often absent for long periods."

Buck's trip to *Javelina* had been successful. Well worth the time and effort to create the party and a modicum of trust with the inhabitants. He now had a possible name for the "Boss" of the cattle rustling and a plan involving the two 'J-H' branded hides.

San Saba Gold

XXVIII

Big Tooth could hear the soldiers coming up the creek toward his hiding place. He thought, *I will chase these ponies toward them and maybe they will chase the ponies. I will remain hidden until they race after the ponies. Then, I will run down the creek away from them and escape.*

Big Tooth removed the horsehair Comanche bridles from the lower jaws of the horses. He took an arrow from his quiver and gave each of them a sharp jab in the rump with the iron tip. The horses bolted away and clattered down the creek bed in the direction of the soldiers.

Bill gave a shout, "Ready, men, here they come! Be careful not to shoot the horses."

Bill reined his horse over to the side of the gully and watched as the two riderless horses thundered past. "After them, men! No one is riding them and we need them back at camp."

Bill let the troopers chase down the horses. He knew that they would quit running soon and the men would catch them easily enough. He eased along the creek bed in search of the two Indians. As he rounded a bend, he spotted the caved in clay bank and recognized it for what it was. *Looks like the one that the Corporal shot is dead and his partner buried him as best he could. I expect that the other one slipped out into the tall grass after he sent the horses back to us. I'll call it even and avoid catching an arrow.*

It was noon before the scout and troopers returned to camp with the recovered two horses. George had the troop packed and ready to move as soon as the men had a hasty meal.

Bill said, "If we head due south, we will strike the Beaver River by late tomorrow afternoon. Then we can follow along the Beaver until she makes a big bend back to the northeast. From there, pritnear a straight shot to the southeast will put us on the Canadian River right about at Adobe Walls. All in all, I figure a week to the trading post. The Beaver is likely dry, but I reckon we can find a spring or two along its course. Then, it'll likely be a dry hump to the Canadian, so we best leave here totin' all the water we can."

The trek to Adobe Walls was dry but uneventful. They found the trading post and saloon abandoned and falling apart. Bill said, "I was here two years ago. The place was swarmin' with buffalo hunters and the saloon was doin' a brisk business. I reckon they all pulled out after that battle with all them Indians. You remember the story about Billy Dixon making that shot that knocked one of the Indians off his horse from a mile away. Lucky shot if you ask me. Anyway, there's no provisions to be had here, as you can see, but we got water down yonder at the river."

George said, "I think we will rest the men and livestock here a few days before moving on. We are out of grain and need to let the animals graze for a bit."

"Yes, Sir," said Bill, "a few days rest and we'll do fine. It's only about two weeks to the town of Albany where we can pick up the cattle trail south. Between here and there, we'll have reliable water every couple of days or so. Albany is a provision stop for the drovers so we can reload on provisions, grain, and whatever repairs we need to the wagons or tack. Once we're on the cattle trail we can make better time on down to San Antone."

George camped the men and wagons a couple of miles west of Albany and rode into town with the scout and Sergeant

O'Halloran who drove the supply wagon. Albany was a beehive of activity or so it seemed after so many days of plodding across the barren landscape. At the mercantile, they loaded canned goods, dried beans, flour, and bacon as well as sacks of grain for the horses and mules. At the livery, George bought three more horses and two mules. These were to replace those of his animals that were in poor condition.

Back at camp, George called all of the men together. He stood on the seat of one of the wagons and said, "Men, we've had a hard pull so far and I plan to write good reports on each one of you. From here on, the going will be easier although we still have a few more weeks to reach our final destination. Tonight, after we have eaten, I want us to have a bit of a celebration. Sergeant O'Halloran has a side of beef for you to cook, and he has a few bottles of fine whiskey for you to pass around. There is to be no fighting, and I want all firearms placed in this wagon. Let's have a bit of fun and then rest here tomorrow. I expect a few of you will have sore heads in the morning. Now, let's rustle up supper!"

The men gave George a rousing cheer and then rushed off to build a cook fire and get supper started. George climbed down off the wagon and walked out to where the horses and mules were grazing. The sun hung huge and red just above the dusty horizon. The southeast breeze was heavy with the smell of cattle. *I guess we will be smelling cattle all the way to Kerrville. But, at least we will be unlikely to meet up with hostile Indians. I need to write a letter to Jenny tonight while the men have their party. I can mail it from Albany tomorrow. I hope that all is well with her and her family. I should send a dispatch to Colonel Morris as well since he has had no contact from me since we left Pueblo.*

By midnight, George could hear nothing from the men but snoring. Two of the men who were abstainers due to their religious beliefs had agreed to stand guard while their comrades had their fun. George sealed the envelopes and stood up from his small writing table. He stepped out of his tent and walked out to where the two guards were positioned.

He coughed to alert them of his presence.

George said, "Men, why don't you go to the campfire and get yourselves some coffee. Private Phillips, hand me your rifle and I'll take a turn as guard while you two take a short break. One of you come back and join me while the other gets a couple of hours of sleep. I'll come wake whichever is first to sleep and can switch with the other. If I get sleepy, I'll get the scout to replace me. He is not much of a whiskey drinker and he'll be okay as a second guard. Besides, I feel that we are reasonably safe this close to town and all the cattlemen in the area."

George awoke to the sound of moaning. At first, he thought some of the men had been injured. He jumped from his cot and stepped outside the tent into the foggy predawn mist. *Well, a few are injured but we were not attacked. Injured by too much whiskey.* He stepped back into his tent and put on his uniform and boots. By the time he was back outside, the sun was just peeking over the eastern horizon. He strode to the campfire and got a cup of coffee. The cooks were frying bacon and heating up a pot of beans. The smell of bacon and coffee brought a few of the men out of their bedrolls. Most of them were up and dragging about the water wagon trying to relieve their whiskey induced thirst.

Sergeant O'Halloran bellowed, "'Mornin', lads! I see you all had a good rest and are ready for a full day in the Texas sunshine. I believe we'll dig us a big pit today just for the fun of it!" He then roared with laughter. "You boys best stay clear of man's drink if it hit you that hard."

XXIX

Buck rode up to the front of the large stone house that served as the headquarters of the J-Bar-H ranch. A young cowboy stepped down from the front gallery. He held a Henry Yellow Boy rifle loosely across his body but pointed just to the left of Buck. He said, "What you doing here, Injun? Yer lucky I didn't shoot yew when yew come through the gate."

Buck slowly dismounted and untied the rolled up cattle hides from behind the cantle of his saddle. He flipped the hides open and onto the ground at the young man's feet. "I reckon from the brands that these came off a couple of your steers. Ain't that so? And, I'm only part Indian."

The rifle muzzle now pointed at the center of Buck's chest. The cowboy gave a loud whistle and then said, "Keep yer hands away from them pistols. Now, where yew git them hides?"

"Careful with that rifle, you might shoot somebody. I sure don't want it to be me," said Buck with a big grin. "You got an owner or a foreman I can talk to about those hides?"

"The Boss ain't here. Jake's the ramrod and he's over at the round pen watchin' our *vaqueros* break some green mustangs."

"Then, what say I mosey over there and see Jake. I'll leave the hides here for now. You can guard them if you like or come with me."

"My orders are to stay here on the porch and guard the house. Here comes Manuel. He heard my whistle. He'll walk yew over to the pens. Leave yer pony here and maybeso put yer gun belt up around yer saddle horn jist so nobody gits shot," he gave his own big grin.

Buck complied with the request and accompanied Manuel to the round pen. A very tall man, who appeared to be forty years or so of age, stood just outside the fence watching a young Mexican on the back of a pitching horse. The rider was good at his job and stuck to the horse like a tick. The horse and rider had kicked up a great deal of the brown dust and at times disappeared in the dust cloud. After a few minutes the horse was worn down and began racing around the inside perimeter of the pen. After a few circuits the Mexican reined him in and walked him over to the fence next to the tall man.

"*Señor* Jake," said the young *vaquero*, "I think this will be a good one. A few more rides and he will be ready for training with the *vacas*."

"Good work, Benito. You can turn him out in the horse trap with the others. I want you to work him again *mañana.*"

Jake turned to face Buck as he walked up and said, "We aren't taking on extra hands right now."

"I am not here for a job," said Buck. "I have brought a couple of hides that I think wear the brand of this ranch. I found two men skinning the steers across the river in Mexico. They ran off with the job half done when I rode upon them. Since they ran, I figured that the beeves were stolen. I finished the job of skinning, saw the brands, and brought the hides here."

"That's a long ride for delivering a couple of hides worth maybe three or four dollars off a couple of two-dollar steers. What do you really want?"

"Well, I'm sorta in the freelance cattle business, and I check with ranchers to see if anybody is interested in buying stock cheap without asking a whole lot of questions. What about this outfit? Any interest in adding to your herd? I see signs that a fair number of cattle move across your spread heading south."

"I run a legit outfit and have no interest in stolen cattle. I suggest that you get off this ranch before I string you up as a rustler."

As Buck rode away from the ranch house he thought, *Well, it looks like the foreman doesn't know what's going on around here. That, or else he's a good liar. Strange the way he looked surprised when I mentioned the signs of cattle moving south across the ranch. Maybe he stays a bit too close to the headquarters to know what is going on around him?*

Buck rode into the dusty little village of Carrizo Springs and tied Patch to an iron ring driven into a big mesquite. At least, there was some shade under the tree. The adobe cantina looked vacant, but as he stepped inside he saw an old man sleeping at a corner table. Buck put his hand on the old man's shoulder and gave it a gentle shake. The man jerked upright so violently that he fell backwards onto the floor. As Buck offered his hand to pull the startled man to his feet, the man cringed back in obvious fear.

"*Usted habla ingles?*" asked Buck. "I mean you no harm. I only want water, *agua.*"

"*Ingles*, a leetle," said the man. "*Hay el agua,*" he said pointing to a bucket sitting at the end of the bar.

Buck scooped up a dipper of water and gave it a sniff. It smelled okay and tasted okay but with a hint of the oak taste from the bucket. After several more drinks he said, "*Gracias*" and reached into his pocket for a coin.

The old man waved the coin away and said, "*Nada por el agua.*"

Buck sat at a table and wrote a short coded message informing Major Jones of his whereabouts and what he had discovered about the rustling operation. Just then, a middle-aged man wearing a forked-tail coat stepped into the cantina. He asked the old man, "Are you coming to the prayer meeting? We need you to play your concertina for the hymns."

Buck realized that the old man understood much more English than he had been led to believe. Buck said to the man in the coat, "Howdy, Preacher, I'm just passing through and need to send off a letter. Is there postal service to this town?"

The Preacher gave Buck a stern look and said, "No, young man. The nearest is post office is in Eagle Pass to the southwest or Uvalde to the north. Eagle Pass is closer, about two days by horseback, but it is a rough town filled with sinners like all towns where the Army has a fort."

"Thanks, Preacher, I'll get started at first light. If anybody needs letters posted, I'd be happy to carry them provided they give me money for the postage. I expect it'll be around six cents for a one-page letter. Leastways, it was the last one I sent."

XXX

The hung-over troopers stumbled about and slowly loaded the wagons for the continuation of the journey south. It was past noon before the caravan set out on the cattle trail south of Albany. That night they camped on the north bank of the nearly dry Hubbard Creek.

Bill rode into camp, dismounted, and said, "Lieutenant, these cattle herds moving north have grazed off pritnear all the grass for two miles either side of the main cow trail. I recommend that we ease off to the west four or five miles and then parallel the trail as we head south. That way we can find graze for our stock and stay mostly upwind of the dust and smell of the herds being driven north."

"Sounds like a good plan to me," replied George. "What say you leave out at first light to map our route and mark good places for us to camp? I anticipate that we will find water more regularly now. Elsewise the drovers would not use this way north."

"Yes, there are a good many creeks and rivers from here on to San Antonio. I see that you have set camp on the north side of this creek. From here on, I recommend that we always cross a creek or river before setting up camp. You never know in this country when a dry creek will suddenly become a raging torrent."

"Good advice and henceforth we will abide your counsel. But for tonight, I see no threat of rain, and the men still need a bit more rest after their frolic in Albany."

★★★

San Saba Gold

George awoke from a restless sleep to a strange sound. Once he had cleared his head of the grogginess of sleep, he realized he was hearing water rushing past in what had been a dry creek bed only hours before. He quickly pulled on his trousers and boots and rushed from his tent. In the bright moonlight, he could see that the creek was running and appeared to be on a rise. *This country is mighty strange, indeed. No sign of a cloud for days and here comes a flood out of nowhere. Well, Bill warned me, sure enough. It will be two good hours until daylight. No sense trying to get across in the dark. We'll just see how deep it is come morning.*

George walked down to the creek bank at first light and attempted to estimate the depth of the rushing yellow-brown water. Bill walked up beside him and handed George a cup of steaming coffee. Bill spoke first and said, "I'd allow it's four to five foot deep out there in the middle where it's runnin' the swiftest. I wouldn't want to swim my horse acrost it unlessen I had Comanches on my tail. Even then, I might stand and fight rather than drown."

George said, "I concur. We will just have to wait for it to run down. Let's go get some breakfast and get the troopers busy hitching the teams and breaking camp. Maybe by the time that all is ready, we can get across."

By mid-morning, the water level had dropped by half and George decided to cross. Though it was a struggle and there were a few dicey moments, they got the supply wagon and the two wagons containing the gold across without mishap. The last to cross was the water wagon and then disaster struck. At mid-stream, one of the mules slipped down and created a jumble of mules, harness, and double trees. The driver jumped down and jerked out the king pin to allow the team to regain footing and prevent further injury to the mules and hitch gear. The tank on the water wagon was nearly empty. The unhitched wagon drifted downstream thirty yards, hit some hidden obstruction, and rolled over. The swift current made short work of the tank and its wagon.

Bill rode his horse over to where George was standing and dismounted. He said, "Lieutenant, it could have been worse. The men are all safe as are the livestock. We will only have a day or two from here south without a stream to camp by. If we had to lose a wagon, that was the best one to let go."

Five days later, Bill said to George, "We'll make Pegleg Crossing on the San Saba tomorrow. Then, it's only about a week to San Antonio. We've made it past the hard parts and just got clear sailin' ahead."

Word spread quickly through the troopers that they were almost to their destination. After supper, George called the men together, climbed up on the seat of the supply wagon, and said, "Men, you have undoubtedly heard that we are little more than a week away from our goal. I want to thank each one of you for your teamwork and dedication to our mission. When we reach San Antonio, I will write a letter of commendation for each one of you to be placed in your record of service. You are a credit to your uniforms. Now, let us get this last short journey done."

The men shouted out a cheer and thanked George for his leadership and Bill for his scouting abilities. George jumped down from the wagon seat and went to his tent where he fetched a bottle of rum that he had hidden in his valise. He walked back to the campfire and said, "Men, hold out your cups. I feel that we should all toast each other for a job well done thus far."

George went among his men and poured a taste into each man's cup. He raised his own cup and announced, "To us."

The cattle trail coursed between cedar-covered hills as

it wound it way to the crossing of the San Saba River. The river ran crystal clear across a white limestone bed at the crossing. Bill said that the Pegleg Crossing was an easy one and had been used to move tens of thousands of cattle north over the last several years.

The troopers on horseback gathered close around the wagons as the caravan eased into the clear, free-flowing water. George held up his hand to halt the procession and said, "Let your horses and mules drink. This looks like some of the best water we have seen since we left Denver. Dismount and fill your canteens. Bill tells me that we only have a few days more on the cattle trail before we can take the San Antonio Road from Kerrville."

Most of the troopers were kneeling at the water's edge filling their canteens when the shooting began. Bill and ten of the troopers were mortally wounded at the first volley. The two surviving teamsters crouched behind one of the wagons and began returning fire. George fired a few shots toward their attackers and heard one cry out as he fell. A shot from the brush hit one of the remaining teamsters in the forehead killing him instantly.

George fired into the brush until his revolver clicked on empty. As he rushed toward the wagon where the remaining teamster was reloading, George was knocked from his horse with a wound to the chest. Corporal Morris ran toward his wounded lieutenant but was cut down with a volley from the attackers.

George lay on his side in the shallow, bloody water and watched as a dozen men swarmed out of the cedar thickets. Two of the men were using crude bows to shoot arrows into the dead and wounded men. Others were busy removing scalps from the bodies.

Why shoot arrows into dead men? George thought. At that moment, an arrow struck him in the chest. He made a deep gasp, and muttered, "Jenny, I ..." Then, the blackness of death closed his eyes forever.

———

Richard Willis

The leader of the attackers said, "Pull that supply wagon up on the bank, pull the wagon covers off of the other two wagons, and put them in the supply wagon. Then set the whole thing on fire. Pile all the saddles and other gear into one of the other two wagons, and load all the soldiers' weapons and ammunition into the other one. Put the bodies of our three dead men in with the weapons and ammunition. We will bury them once we are well away from here. Then, shoot a couple of those mules and carve off a hindquarter or two. We want his to look as much like an Indian attack as we can."

"Okay, whip up those teams and let's ride south. As soon as we clear these hills, I want us to get well to the west of this cattle trail. We are too likely to run into a herd or two moving north, and I don't want a bunch of drovers telling tales about a bunch of riders and two wagons heading south."

XXXI

Buck rode into the dusty border town of Eagle Pass, Texas. He dismounted at the front of the livery, looped Patch's reins over a hitching rail, and walked into the barn. A barrel-chested, bald-headed man was bent over shoeing a grulla gelding.

Buck coughed to make his presence known and then asked, "This your outfit here?"

The man dropped the gelding's hoof, stood up, and said, "Yepper, you lookin' to board that Paint stallion you rode in on?"

"Yes, I'd like to leave him here. Please, give him a good rub down and a bait of grain. I rode him hard to get here from Carrizo Springs in a day, and we're both pritnear tuckered. Where's the post office? I've got some letters to mail."

"Them letters must be awful important if'n you pushed that hard from Carrizo. The postal is down yonder at the C&C Mercantile, but if'n your messages is so all fire important to dern near kill your stallion, you might want to go over to the soldier fort. They got one o' them new fangled telly grafs."

Buck thanked the liveryman for the information and paid him for the livery fee. He hitched up his britches and walked out into the dusty street. Most of the town consisted of adobe huts and a few slapped together wooden buildings. The C&C Mercantile looked to be the second most prosperous structure. The Eagle's Nest Saloon topped it for first place.

Buck stepped up onto the rough-hewn boardwalk and entered the Mercantile. The place was crowded with all sorts of goods and ranching equipment. A short, black-haired man wearing a stripped shirt was behind the counter helping an elderly Mexican woman decide on which bolt of fabric she wanted to buy. Buck picked out a new shirt and a pair of canvas pants, then stood behind the old woman.

The storekeeper said, "*Excúseme, Señora* Hernandez." He looked at Buck and asked, "You want anything else besides that shirt and those britches?"

"Yes, I need a box of .44 caliber cartridges and I've got a letter to mail."

Just then, there was a clatter from some odd looking gadget on a desk at the end of the counter. Buck jumped to one side of the old lady and drew his pistol. Once he saw that there was no threat he said, "Sorry, folks. I didn't mean to scare you but that chattering contraption caught me unawares."

The storekeeper chuckled and said, "That there is the telegraph. They strung the wires to the fort last year and spliced us into it as well."

"Good, that'll save me a trip out to the fort. I still want to post my letter. I have a few that the folks in Carrizo wanted me to post for them. Then, I want to send a message to Austin on that clicker gadget of yours."

"Well, we have to charge by the word on the telegraph, so keep your message as short as possible. Otherwise, it'll cost you an arm and a leg. We charge two bits for every hundred miles to send a message of ten words or less. It's about two hundred miles to Austin by way of San Antone, so that'll run you fifty cents for each ten words. I'd make it short."

Buck said, "Let me work on my message and I'll be back, but I still want to post these letters."

After Buck paid for the postage and his purchases, he stepped outside and sat down on a bench against the front wall of the store. *Let's see how I can shorten this message to the Major and stay in code.*

He worked and reworked his message and finally settled on:

———

'Jacob Jones, Good progress, likely head found. Mike.'

Buck walked back inside and handed the storekeeper his note and six bits.

"You want to wait for a reply?"

"No, thanks. It'll likely be a few days before he sends anything back, and I need to get back to the ranch where I work."

After a trip to the local barbershop for a bath and a shave, Buck dressed in his new clothes and went over to the Eagle's Nest for a meal and a beer. The barber had wanted to cut Buck's long hair, but Buck had decided to keep it long for now.

Buck sat at a table in the back corner of the saloon and sipped at his beer. The steak had been a bit tough, but he was hungry enough to chew his way through it anyway. Three grubby looking men and a dark *vaquero* sat at a table midway between Buck and the front of the room.

As they drank their way to the bottom of the bottle of whiskey they had ordered, their voices became loud enough for Buck to overhear their conversation.

"Why did we git left behind? I heard Bob Clarke pick out a dozen hands and tell them that the big Boss had a special job for them. He said there would be a big payday if they did as told and kept their mouths shut. We're gittin' cut outta a big piece of coin, sounds like to me. And, that foreman, Jake, had us gather a herd of steers to move north and then sent us over here to deliver some mail. We won't see any money from the trail drive neither."

The *vaquero* spoke up, "Louie, you got a big mouth and everyone knows it. Right now you need to keep your voice down. That *hombre* in the corner can hear everything you are saying. Besides, Mister Jake will take care of us. He always has."

Buck set his beer mug down on the table and walked to the bar. He put a few coins down to pay for his meal and drink before walking out the front door. *I best gather up Patch and head back over to that J-Bar-H outfit. Two of those fellers were riding drag with that herd heading to Mexico a few weeks back. I reckon that the Boss mentioned was the one I heard about over at the ranch. Likely he's either that Hartright the Mexican in Javelina mentioned or maybe that foreman, Jake.*

XXXII

The morning after the massacre at Pegleg Crossing, John Patterson topped a little rise just south of the San Saba River. In the distance, he saw a spiraling column of vultures. *Must be something dead up near the crossing. I hope the water isn't fouled. My herd will be thirsty after a day and a half from the Llano.*

John's men were a day behind him driving a herd of three thousand longhorns north. He had ridden ahead to scout for grass between the crossing of the Llano River and Pegleg Crossing on the San Saba.

John lightly gigged his spurs into his horse's flanks. When he reached the river, John reined up short. *My God! Indians have massacred a soldier troop. I had best ride hard to Menardville and report this to the local sheriff. He can send someone to alert the military at Fort McKavett so I can get back to my herd.*

The Boss kept his bandana tied across his face. None of his men knew his identity though he suspected that Bob Clarke had puzzled it out. "You men be careful with those wagons. Those weapons and that equipment will bring a good price down across the border. Don Mendoza's silver will fill your pockets. He is planning to build himself a bit on an army. I want to be in Mendoza's debt so all of the money he pays for this shipment will be split among you. I only want for him to owe me future favors when he succeeds in his dream of creating a new country in northern Mexico. He told me that he would call it *República de Coahuila y Leon.*"

Of course, the Boss knew that the weapons and equipment were merely window dressing. He had learned of the true value of the shipment through entertaining a Congressional Aide while in Washington City. The Aide's weakness for expensive Scotch whisky had loosened his tongue just enough. The Boss had hired a private detective to determine the route of the shipment. The detective had determined that the shipment by rail was a ruse and the true shipment was by wagon down the Western Cattle Trail. Don Mendoza may or may not be successful in creating a Presidency for himself but, in any case, being in his good graces would not hurt.

The Pegleg Crossing on the San Saba was ideal for his plan. It was far enough away from his ranch to prevent anyone from suspecting him and far enough from any town to make it unlikely that anyone would hear the gunshots. Also, the ten to twelve day trip down to the ranch would be relatively easy and would cross virtually unpopulated country.

The outlaws' trip south was relatively uneventful. They buried their dead out in the scrub brush the day after the attack. Then, they rode their horses back and forth across the graves so that no evidence of the burials would be discovered. After several days, they crossed the Lower San Antonio to El Paso Road just west of the little village of Sabinal.

The Boss said, "Bob, you and your men hide the wagons in this cedar thicket, make camp, and wait for me to return. I'll ride into Sabinal and buy a wagon to shift all this gear into. I don't want someone who might be looking for two Army wagons to see us with these. I should be back by sundown tomorrow. Oh, and no fires. Smoke would give us away to any folks travelling the road."

True to his word, the Boss arrived late the next afternoon driving a big freight wagon. His horse was tethered behind. He had pulled his bandana up to cover his lower face just before pulling into camp.

He climbed down from the wagon seat and shouted, "Move all of that gear from those two Army wagons into this big freight wagon. Bob, you and your men can take the freight wagon loaded with plunder down to Don Mendoza in Old Mexico. He will be happy to give you a good price. You can divide the money between yourself and your men as you see fit. Bob, pick one of your men to go with me. Tell him that he will get his share of whatever you collect. He and I will drive the two Army wagons well away from here before we take care of destroying them and mules."

Bob said, "Yes, sir, we'll see to it. Should we meet you back at the J-Bar-H or what once we are finished with Don Mendoza?"

"No, once you have finished your business, why not take the boys to San Antonio for a bit of a frolic. Then, see if you can gather another herd from the Nueces River ranchers to move south. The owner of the J-Bar-H sent Jake and the *vaqueros* off to drive a herd of J-Bar-H steers north to the buyers in Kansas. As you may know, the owner of this ranch is often away for months at a time. No one else is there except for the house servants, and they know to mind their own business. Now get a move on. You have a good six hours of sunlight left. *Adios.*"

Buck rode at a leisurely pace back to the J-Bar-H. "Patch, old boy, I think that there is something more to be learned back at that ranch." *Lord, here I am talking to my horse. I must be going loco. He didn't even twitch and ear so he's ignoring me. I need to wrap this project up and get back to the Rangers. I believe I'll go ahead and muster out so I can go back to the Nations and Becky.*

Although a longer route than the one he had taken from Carrizo Springs to Eagle Pass, the trail along the north bank of the Rio Grande would eventually lead Buck back to where the J-Bar-H bordered the river. And, it had the advantages of ready access to water and an occasional small village where he might find a meal either on the Mexico side of the river or on the Texas side.

When Buck reached the wide north-to-south cattle trail used by the rustlers, he knew he was back on J-Bar-H land. He turned Patch north and headed for ranch headquarters. The dense walls of brush on either side of the trail were at least seven feet tall, which made it impossible for Buck to get sight of the ranch headquarters.

After he had travelled approximately ten miles from the river, he found a large live oak tree near the edge of the trail. By standing on his saddle atop Patch's back, he was able to pull himself up onto a large limb and then climb farther up into the tree. Off to the northeast a couple of miles across the brush, he could see smoke rising from a chimney. *That's got to be the cookhouse back behind ranch headquarters. It's too derned hot for anybody to be burning a fire in a fireplace inside the house,* he thought.

Although the brush was dense, there were occasional small trails into the thickets. Here and there, the trails opened into clearings of an acre or so. Most clearings were created by Longhorn bulls during their dominance battles. The wild Longhorn bulls would tear up the ground both during their pre-battle displays of pawing up the ground and flinging dirt and brush over their backs, as well as during the sparing contests. Mature bulls weigh nearly a ton each. Two tons of enraged bulls battling over rights to the cows can clear out a goodly piece of brush.

Buck turned Patch onto a trail into the brush. He slipped his bow from its buckskin case and strung it. Then, he chose one of his arrows. He dismounted and tied Patch's reins to a huisache limb. He eased down the trail hoping to surprise a deer or a javelina. The trail ahead curved around a large mesquite. Buck stopped behind the tree and peeked into the little clearing beyond. An armadillo was rooting around along the south edge of the clearing, and a spike buck was grazing on the weeds growing out in the middle.

The setting sun was at Buck's back and a gentle breeze blew toward him. As long as he moved only when the buck's head was down eating, he should be undetected. Buck nocked an arrow into his bowstring, drew the bow, eased from behind the tree, and let the arrow fly. The young buck jumped at the strike of the arrow, took a couple of bounds toward the trail to the east, and then fell dead. Buck's arrow had passed completely through the deer and sailed off into the dense brush. It was not worth being chewed up by the thorny brush to look for it.

Buck walked back to where Patch had been tied and climbed into the saddle. As he rode into the clearing, he loosened the pigging string that held his rawhide *riata*. He dismounted near the dead deer and looped a noose around the deer's hind legs, remounted Patch, dallied the *riata* around his saddle horn, and then used Patch to drag the deer back to the big mesquite.

It was full dark by the time Buck had skinned and butchered the deer. He had hobbled Patch and let him graze out in the meadow.

Buck dug a hole down into the sandy soil and built a fire in it. No one would be able to see the light of his fire and the smoke would drift off to the west – away from the ranch headquarters. He speared a healthy chunk of backstrap onto a stick that he angled above the fire. His mouth watered as the aroma of the roasting meat wafted his way.

He salted the rest of the meat and wrapped it in the deer's hide. Then, he hung the parcel from a limb of the big mesquite so that coyotes and other varmints could not get at it. He had already carried the parts of the deer that he did not want well away from his little campsite. He could already hear raccoons bickering over the remains. After he had eaten, he shoveled the pile of dirt next to the hole back over the dying coals of his fire and settled into his blanket.

The Boss said, "Hector, tie your pony to the back of that wagon. You drive that one and I'll drive this one. Now follow me."

"*Si, Señor,*" said Hector. He knew better than to ask any questions about why the Boss wanted these wagons and the nature of their destination.

Three days later, they were well within the northern portion of the J-Bar-H when the Boss reined his team to a stop and climbed down off the wagon. He stepped to the side of the dirt road as if he planned to relieve his bladder.

Hector wrapped his reins around the brake handle and was just climbing down from the wagon when a pistol shot to his head killed him instantly. The Boss dropped his revolver into its holster and walked over to Hector's body. *No witnesses from here on,* he thought. He used Hector's pony to drag the body well away from the road into the brush. *Coyotes and buzzards will clean him up soon enough.*

After retying Hector's saddle pony and his own horse to the back of Hector's wagon, he unhitched the team from the wagon and led them off into the brush on the opposite side of the road from where he had dragged Hector's body. He killed both mules and cut away the hide on their hips bearing the incriminating 'US' brands. He dragged the harness back to the road and threw it up into the wagon he had been driving. He lashed Hector's wagon tongue to the back of his wagon and climbed back aboard. *Not but a couple of miles back to the barn. I'll get there before dark.*

XXXIII

John Patterson was just a few miles from reaching Menardville when he was met by six heavily armed men on horseback. He recognized one of them as a Texas Ranger he had seen in Kerrville and judged the rest of the men to be Rangers as well. He reined up and raised his right hand in greeting. "Are you boys all Rangers?"

"Yes, sir," said the man who appeared to be in charge. "I am Sergeant Jones. Do you have business with us?"

"My name is John Patterson. I was on my way to Menardville to report a massacre of some Yankee soldiers back at Pegleg Crossing. They are all dead and shot full of holes with both bullets and arrows. Even their livestock is dead. My men and I are moving a herd north, and I came across the dead men at the river crossing. I really need to get back to my herd. Can you send one of your men to the soldier fort to alert them?"

"Willie, you ride back to Fort McKavett and tell the Post Commander what this man told us. Mr. Patterson, the rest of us will ride with you back to the scene and try to determine where the Indians went. It's strange though since we have no reports of raids around here for the last several months."

Buck stood in the shadows of the big barn. He had penned Patch in a small clearing in the dense brush by using thorny brush to close off the narrow trail into the clearing. He stashed his saddle and bridle up in a large huisache tree and walked the mile or so to ranch headquarters. When he arrived, he found the place fairly deserted except for three Mexican women gossiping in the main house. He was careful that they did not see him. He was searching the barn when he heard a wagon rumbling down the road leading to the headquarters buildings. After scrambling up the ladder into the hayloft, he hid near the front loft door.

As the wagon approached the barn, Buck eased back into a corner and concealed himself behind a stack of sacked grain. He could see that a man had driven a double wagon hitch into the barn. Two saddled horses were tethered to the rear of the second wagon. The man unhitched the mule team from the wagon and led them out the back of the barn.

In a few minutes, the man returned untied one of the saddled horses and led it out to where the mules were standing. The man returned to the barn, removed the saddle from the second horse, led it out to the corral next to the barn, and slipped off the bridle.

In the meantime, Buck had moved to the back of the barn loft where he could watch the man through a crack between two of the boards in the loft wall. The man removed the harness from the mules and hung it on a nearby corral fence. He then tied the mules head-to-tail, mounted the horse, and rode south leading the mules.

After waiting about ten minutes, Buck climbed down the ladder and inspected the two wagons. He could see nothing unusual in the dim light of the barn, especially since the sun was beginning to set. As he was examining the bed of one of the wagons, he heard two rifle shots off to the south. He quickly jumped down from the wagon bed and climbed back into the hayloft.

Shortly, he heard the sound of a horse trotting back toward the barn and soon spotted the man he had seen earlier. *Reckon he shot those mules? Why on earth would a man shoot two perfectly good mules?*

The man rode up to the corral behind the barn, unsaddled the horse, and closed him inside the corral. After hanging the saddle and bridle in the tack room, the man slid the barn doors closed and walked to the large ranch house, which he entered.

Buck heard a woman exclaim, "*Hola, Señor,* you are home. Do you want something to eat?"

Buck could hear the man mumble an indistinct reply, but the distance was too great for him to hear more. He climbed down the ladder to the barn floor and eased the back barn door open enough to slip out. After closing the door, he walked around the corral and into the night.

Buck's curiosity about the mules made him decide to investigate before returning to Patch and his makeshift camp. He was pretty certain that the darkness would prevent anyone from the house spotting him but did not walk directly toward the trail that the man had led the mules down. Instead, he walked west to the brush line. Then, using the brush as a backdrop so that he would not be easily seen, he worked his way back to the trail.

The dead mules were in a little clearing about a half mile from where Buck entered the trail. There was enough moonlight for Buck to see that the man had cut away the brand from each mule's hip. And, from the size of the place where the hide had been cut away, the brand was a big one. None of the hundreds of brands that Buck had recorded in his mission was nearly that large. *What in the hell could those brands have been and why would the man remove them? In fact, why kill the derned mules? Why not just run them across the river and let the Mexicans have them?*

As Buck worked his way back to check on Patch and have something to eat, he puzzled, *There's something very odd about all of this and it ain't likely to have anything to do with cattle rustling. I best get Patch to some water, pen him back up, and have me a quick cold supper. I'll catch a bit of a nap then get back to that barn and have a better look at those wagons before sunup.*

San Saba Gold

Buck dared not risk a light and the closed up barn was too dark for him to see much. He climbed up into the wagon box of the first wagon and got down on his hands and knees so that he could feel around the edges of the box. Up at the front of the box just below the seat, he felt a small, round, domed disk. He sat up and tried to see what it was but it was too dark to see. As he felt the disk on both sides, he smiled. *Why, I believe it's a brass button.* He stuck it into his shirt pocket and continued his search. There was nothing else to be found so he climbed down and proceeded to the second wagon. At the front of the wagon box he found three cartridge casings. He stuck them into his pocket as well. He heard a male Cardinal calling followed immediately by crowing of a rooster. *Must be getting light outside. I best get back up in the loft and see what develops, if anything.*

Buck sat on a short stack of feed sacks in one corner of the loft. He had drifted into a light sleep when the sound of the big barn door sliding open brought him awake with a start.

The man Buck had seen yesterday walked around the wagons carefully looking them over. He then walked to the far end of the barn and opened the wooden door of a small storage room. He entered the little room and banged around in there. When he reemerged, he was carrying a small sledgehammer, an ax, and a crowbar.

Just then a Mexican woman shouted, "*Patron,* the breakfast is ready."

The man hung the crowbar on the side of the first wagon's box and dropped in the sledgehammer and ax. He then left the barn and strolled back to the house.

Buck stood and stretched. He reached into his pocket and extracted the shell casings and button. The button was from a cavalry enlisted man's shirt. The shell casings were stamped '45-70 GOVT'. *Army stuff. These must be Army wagons and that's why the brands were cut off the mules.*

They were Army mules. These wagons have to have been stolen. What's that jaybird planning to do with those wrecking tools?

Buck quickly climbed down the loft ladder and took a closer look at the wagons. Both had what appeared to be several places where bullets had struck the boards along the sides of the wagons. *Now that's odd. The floors inside these wagon boxes are a good six inches higher than the lower board edge on the sides. It looks like there's a false bottom in both of these wagons. And, unless I miss my bet, these are U.S. Army wagons. Likely that feller is planning to rip up the false bottoms to get at whatever's under there.*

Buck heard someone approaching the barn whistling a lively tune. Buck scrambled back up into the loft just before the man stepped into the barn.

Buck lay prone on the loft floor peeking through a crack between boards. The man pulled the barn door closed behind him and climbed up into the first wagon. He used the ax to chop into the wagon floor and then the crowbar to pry up a couple of the floorboards. As the man cleared away more of the false floor, Buck could see what appeared to be trays with big brass washers stacked on edge in the trays.

The man bent down and pulled out one of the washers. When the man held the washer up to give it a careful look, Buck gasped as he saw that it was not a washer but a gold coin. *Looks like a Yankee Double Eagle,* Buck thought. *Lord Almighty, if both wagons are full of those coins, there is a fortune down there. Stolen, no doubt.*

Buck eased his revolver from his holster and tried to quietly creep over to the ladder but a creaking board gave him away. The man below dropped the coin, looked up abruptly, and shouted, "Who's up there? Show yourself."

Buck stepped to the ladder opening and said in a loud voice, "Put your hands on top of your head. I'm a Texas Ranger and I want to know what you are doing with all that Yankee gold."

Immediately, the man jumped out of the wagon bed and

dropped behind the front wheel. Buck could no longer see him so he started down the ladder. Climbing down was awkward since he had his revolver in his right hand as he descended the ladder facing away from it. He dared not turn his back on the man who might have a gun of his own.

Buck was halfway down the ladder when the man popped up from behind the wagon and hurled the short handled sledgehammer at Buck. The hammer struck Buck just below his sternum and knocked the wind out of him. He dropped his revolver as he fell to the barn floor. Meanwhile, the man ran from the barn toward the house. As Buck struggled to regain the ability to breathe, he realized that the man would quickly return with a gun and kill him if he remained lying helplessly in the dirt.

XXXIV

John Patterson and the Rangers arrived at Pegleg Crossing just ahead of John's herd of cattle. Sergeant Jones said, "Mr. Patterson, get your men to hold up your herd."

"Sergeant, those cattle are thirsty and they will smell water, if they haven't already. There won't be any way we can hold them back."

"Well then, haze them over to that little creek that feeds into the river. Looks to me like there's enough water to keep them steers occupied until we can see what happened here."

John Patterson rode off south to his herd as Sergeant Jones turned to his men, "Boys, I'm fixin' to go on down to the river and see what I can find out. Y'all circle out and see what sorta tracks you can find. If it was Injuns, their ponies will be unshod. Of course, y'all know that. Anyways, see what you can find."

After scouting the surrounding area, the Rangers met with Sergeant Jones a couple of hundred yards south of the river crossing. Private Lewis said, "Sarge, don't you think we oughta bury them soldier boys? They're pretty ripe and the varmints have been at them."

"Nope, the Yankee Army will be here directly with Willie. They would pitch a hissy fit if we moved the bodies afore they had their look see. Of course, I doubt they could find a buffalo in a pool hall, but we'll let them tidy up their dead. We'll make our little report to whatever officer shows up and then get on the trail of whoever done this. From what y'all found and from the looks of the arrows stuck in them bodies, I'm fair certain it warn't no Injuns what did this."

A half-hour later, the Rangers heard the clatter and jingle that only the U.S. Cavalry could make. In a few minutes, a dozen of the boys in blue rode up with Willie and a very young lieutenant in the lead. As the column came to a halt, Willie said, "Sarge, this here's Lieutenant Baldwin fresh out here to Texas from the east. He's in charge of this soldier patrol. Seems he was a lawman of some sort back in Boston afore he joined the Army."

"Thank you, William," said the Lieutenant. Then to Sergeant Jones he said, "My troops and I will be taking over the investigation from here on. I sincerely hope that you and your men have not spoiled the crime scene."

"Well, soldier boy, we have been solving crimes for years while you soldier boys have been shining your buttons and practicin' parades. We ain't messed up YOUR crime scene, but the buzzards, coyotes, and other varmints may have sullied things a might. Here's what I know. This here arrow warn't made by no Injun, leastwise not one from this part of the country. Our Injuns are pritnear particular about how they dress up their arrows, and a war party don't use no hunting arrow points. They use war points. On top of that, our Injuns are pritnear whipped and they sure don't steal no wagons. An Injun's got as much use for a wagon as a pig's got for a parasol."

Sergeant Jones turned to his men and said, "Come on, boys, the Army is in charge of this mess. Mount up and let's git. We need to cover some ground if we want to make it to Mason by noon tomorrow. We can camp tonight somewhere along the way. I need to send a telegraph to Austin about this soldier massacre. That one dead soldier had a bit of a journal in his pocket. They come down here all the way from Denver. Musta been a real important reason for a bunch of Army boys to be driving wagons that far."

★★★

Buck had had the helpless feeling of having his wind knocked out of him a couple of times in the past when he was bucked from horses. At one level, Buck knew that he just needed to relax and his breathing would restart, but knowing it and living through it were two different things. Plus, if he did not get up and regain his composure quickly, he would be easy prey when the man returned. Suddenly, he gasped a deep breath. He took a few more breaths and rolled over onto his belly. Lord, but his abdomen hurt where the hammer hit him. He picked up his revolver and scrambled to his feet. *Boy, Howdy! I sure wish I had my Winchester.* Buck had left his saddle gun and Colt revolver back at his camp.

From just outside the open barn door, a shotgun boomed. A load of double-ought buckshot slammed into the wagon just to the left of where Buck stood. Wood splinters flew just past Buck's head. He jumped across the barn aisle and flattened himself against a stall door.

The shotgun boomed again and more wood splintered from the wagon. One of the double-ought pellets ricocheted off the wagon's front wheel rim and popped Buck in the right thigh. He could feel blood running down his leg into his boot. A double-ought pellet is the diameter of a .33 caliber bullet, so while it makes a sizeable hole, much of the force had been dissipated by the strike on the steel wagon tire. *Well, I ain't dead yet and I don't think I'm hit too bad. Hurts like blazes but I'll tend to it later.*

Buck sidled toward the back door of the barn. Between the deep bruise below his breastbone and the ball in his thigh, he thought that he might black out.

He heard the man reloading the scattergun, so he fired a shot in the direction of the sound, then ducked out of the door and moved to the side. Just in time, too, as the shotgun boomed again.

Buck bluffed, "You best give up, the rest of my Rangers will have heard the shots and be swarming over you any minute."

Buck reached down and gave the wound on his thigh a

firm squeeze. He felt the lead ball pop out and roll down his pants leg and into his boot. *Great, shot in the leg, belly bashed up, and now I got to get my boot off before that ball works its way under my foot.*

Buck eased along the back wall of the barn and sat down on a nail keg to remove his boot. He shook out the pellet and saw that there was not too much blood in the boot. Just as he was stuffing his foot back into the boot, he heard the creak of a wooden door inside the barn. *Likely he's grabbing a saddle and bridle from that tack room and will be heading for one of those horses in the corral.*

Buck stood and then staggered as vertigo caused him to fall against the barn wall. He dropped to his hands and knees as a shotgun blast tore through the wall where he had stood only a moment before. Buck slumped to the ground and let out a moan as his bruised abdomen landed on an apple-sized stone.

The man inside the barn scampered out the front door and ran for the corral. Buck thought, *He figured he got me with that last shot and now will be on the run since he thinks more Rangers are coming.*

Buck pushed himself to his feet and held onto the barn wall as he tried to clear his head. He heard the man gallop away to the west. *I've got to get to Patch and get after him.*

Buck dropped his revolver back into its holster after replacing the spent shells with new ones. He unbuckled his gun belt and set it on the nail keg. Then, he unbuckled his belt and lowered his pants in order to assess the damage to his leg. The wound was weeping a bit but the blood flow had pretty much stopped. The leg was beginning to swell around the wound. *Well, coulda been worse. A few inches higher and he would have gelded me.* He mopped at the wound with his sweat soaked bandana and pulled up his pants. He rebuckled the pants and gun belt and pushed away from the barn wall.

He took a few limping steps in the direction where he had left his horse then stopped. *What am I thinking? I got a good look at him and can catch him later. I'd best secure the gold in those wagons first.*

Buck hobbled back to the barn and looked into the wagon with the false floor removed. He picked up the man's ax and walked to the second wagon. A couple of blows with the ax revealed that this wagon also contained trays of gold coins. *I sure as hell can't drive two wagons and there ain't a team of mules or horses handy. That man took both of the horses from the corral with him to keep me from following. Maybe I can get Patch to pull one of the wagons. He ain't goin' to like it but I reckon I can give it a try.*

In Austin, a clerk knocked on Texas Adjutant Steele's office door and stepped inside. "General, a Ranger Sergeant name of Jones just sent this wire from Mason. Looks like somebody killed a bunch of Army soldiers up on the San Saba and stole a couple of wagons."

"Let me see that," said General Steele as the young man handed over the telegram.

After reading the message, the General wrote out a note and handed it to the clerk. "Take that over to the telegrapher and have him send it to the Office of the Secretary of War in Washington City. Wait for a reply."

The clerk took the folded piece of paper and rushed out of the office. As he walked briskly down the hall, he unfolded the paper to see what it said.

"ARMY TROOPS KILLED BY UNKNOWN PARTIES. WAGONS STOLEN. DO YOU REQUIRE ASSISTANCE FROM US?"

Two hours later, an Army Captain was ushered into General Steele's office. "Sir, I am Captain Art Sims. I have been ordered to inform you that the murdered detachment was on a secret mission to deliver one hundred fifty thousand in gold coin to San Antonio for the construction of the new fort there."

General Steele interrupted, "Sounds like your secret wasn't so secret, was it?"

"Sir, regardless, I have been ordered to request your assistance in recovering the gold and apprehending the thieves."

"Very good, I'll have my Rangers give it top priority. Who will serve as liaison from the Army side?"

"I will, Sir."

"Let my clerk know where you can be reached. I will be in touch as soon as I have any information for you. Keep my clerk informed of anything helpful that your people find. And, please ask my clerk to step in as you leave."

General Steele handed a folded slip of paper to his clerk and said, "Sam, get this message to Major Jones pronto. He should be at Company F in Kerrville by now."

XXXV

Becky sat at the kitchen table peeling apples for a pie while her mother was rolling out dough for a crust.

Mr. Griffin came in through the back door and said, "I was just over to Luke's store, and a fellow came in and told us that DuRant's Store over in Durant Station was robbed and old Mr. DuRant was knocked on the head. The fellow said that Mr. DuRant was home in bed but expected to recover. Seems to me that it's about time we got us a town Marshal again. Ever since Johnny Wilson got married and gave up the job so's he could start farming, the town has gone without."

Mrs. Griffin said, "Now, Papa, that's for the town folks to decide. We country people don't have a say so in what they decide in town. The U.S. Marshal's Office way over yonder in Fort Smith don't give much of a hoot on what happens way down here. I reckon the crooks will just go their merry way."

Becky put down her paring knife and said, "The menfolk around here could do something if they had a mind to. Somebody surely got a look at the crooks. If they are from around these parts, their names are known."

Mr. Griffin said, "I expect that they are some of that trash that lives down there across the river in Texas. They know that the other Texans don't much care what happens up here in the Nations. They are safe as long as they behave south of the river. And, if we were to send men down there after them, the Texans would hang our people for sure."

Becky said, "Well, it's still a pity."

Mrs. Griffin said, "Enough bad news. Becky, are you done with the peeling? I want to get this pie in the oven."

San Saba Gold

Jake and Lem Perkins splashed across the Red River and into Texas. The older brother spoke up, "See there, Lem, I tolt you they didn't have no lawmen over yonder. Did you see the look in that feller's eyes when I give him that first conk? It took two good whacks to lay him out."

"Well, Jake, we only got twelve dollars and a couple of air tights of peaches. Lucky you didn't kill that old man or the Federal Marshal would be prowlin' around since he was a white man."

"Why them lawmen over to Fort Smith ain't worried about a storekeep who got thumped, dead or not. Plus, you heard that feller talk. He's a Frenchman fer sartain. Likely married into that tribe of Injuns, elsewise they wouldn't have let him set up in their area."

"I reckon we oughter stay out of that little town for a spell. I heard one of the Potts boys say there was a store run by an Injun over by the Washita River a bit west of Durant Station. Now, you know fer sure that no lawman from Fort Smith will pay no never mind to a Injun store what gets robbed."

***

Becky walked into Luke's store with a list in her hand. "Luke, Momma needs these things and Papa wants to order two sacks of feed for his mules. Just put Momma's things on our account. Papa said he will pay you when he comes by tomorrow to pick up the feed."

Luke looked at her list and said, "It will take me a few minutes to get your order pulled together. Do you want to browse though the fabric rolls? I got some new ones in since the last time you were in."

"No, thanks. It's a nice day. I'll just sit out front on the bench. I'm in no particular hurry."

Becky sat watching a wren flipping over leaves hunting for insects. She smiled when she saw the little bird take flight with a small caterpillar in her beak. She yawned and stretched and stood as she heard Luke call her name. She turned to look back as she was entering the door. Two scruffy looking men were riding up toward the front of the store.

"Your order is ready. I loaded it into your basket. Want me to put it in the buggy for you?"

"Luke, I'm not some worn out old lady. Here, I'll take it myself. Papa will see you tomorrow about that feed and to settle up our account. Thanks, Luke. Tell Sarah hello for me when you see her."

Becky put her basket behind the seat of the buggy and climbed aboard. As she drove off, the two men she had seen earlier dismounted and looped their reins over the hitching rail in front of the store. The older one had a jagged scar running down from the corner of his left eye to his jaw just beyond his mouth. The younger one had unusual eyes. They were so pale blue that they appeared almost white. Of course, all her Choctaw friends and relatives had dark brown eyes and Buck's eyes were a deep blue. *Oh well, there are all sorts of people. I sure met a bunch of different types down there in Texas.*

Becky was a half-mile down the road when she heard a gun shot. She wasn't sure but it sounded like it came from behind her. The sound of someone shootin a gun was not all that uncommon. It wasn't the season for hunting nor shooting a hog before butchering. Somebody could have been shooting a varmint after their chickens. Still, Becky had a funny feeling about those two men back at Luke's store. Up ahead there was a wide spot in the road where she could turn the buggy around. *If I don't go back and check on Luke, I won't sleep tonight. Probably a waste of time but I have nothing much to do when I get back home.*

Becky had covered only half the distance back to the store when the two scruffy men came galloping toward her. She did not have her revolver with her. Becky never carried it since returning from Texas, but she felt that these men were up to no good. And, she knew that they knew she had seen them at the store.

Becky grabbed the buggy whip out of its bracket next to her right knee and gave 'Sandy' a sharp whap on his hip. The horse was unused to the whip and bolted ahead. Becky and her buggy streaked between the two startled men causing one of the men's horses to rear and crow hop. The rider lost his seat and was tossed.

"Git back on your horse, you ijit! That Injun gal has seen us. Let's get after her. Why'd you have to go and shoot that storekeeper? These Injuns will get riled up and hunt us down if'n that gal ain't stopped."

XXXVI

Buck transferred the trays of coins from the second wagon to the bed of the first. He retrieved a set of harness from the tack room and pitched it into the wagon bed. He added some empty feed sacks and a shovel to the load. He tried to push the heavy wagon out of the barn but the ground was too soft and his injured leg was giving him fits. *Well, nothing to it -- I've got to go get Patch and my stuff. That fellow may decide to come back, and those servants in the house are bound to be curious after all the shooting out here. I need to hurry.*

Buck painfully climbed back up into the loft and threw down a good bit of hay. After climbing back down, he covered the trays of coins with the hay in case anyone from the house came to have a look. Then, he hobbled off across the pasture toward where he had left his horse.

He rode Patch up to the barn and dismounted. His leg and belly still hurt, but the bleeding from his thigh had almost stopped. It did not appear that anyone had been in the barn while he was away.

Now came the tricky part. "Patch, old pardner, this is going to be something new and I expect that you won't like it but bear with me."

Buck had searched the barn thoroughly but the only rig for the wagon was a two-horse hitch. He managed to back Patch up to the wagon but the horse fought the harness and, with only one horse, the tongue swung over into Patch's legs. *Hell's bells, this ain't going to work.*

Buck removed the harness and resaddled the horse. He pulled the tongue pin and put it and the tongue aside.

Then, he lashed the front bolster on each side to the rear bolster so that the front wheels would remain straight. He tied one end of his *riata* through the tongue-pin hole and dallied the other end hard and fast to his saddle horn. He remounted and said, "Come on, boy, this won't be as bad. Now let's pull this wagon."

It was damned unwieldy but it worked with occasional stops to readjust. He hid the wagon in the brush a mile south of the barn and then backtracked on foot sweeping out the tracks with a couple of branches of brush.

When he returned to the wagon, he took the shovel out of the wagon bed and remounted Patch. He followed a game trail through the brush and looked for a good spot to hide the gold. He was certain that the man had not come by all those coins honestly. After an hour, he came to a little side trail that led off to the east. A few hundred yards into the brush, the little trail ended at a large Live Oak. *Good a spot as any.*

He stepped off thirty paces back up the little trail and commenced digging. The sandy brown soil was nearly rock hard. It took Buck two hours of hard work to dig a four-foot deep hole that was wide enough to hold the coins.

Back at the wagon, he transferred the coins to the ten burlap feed sacks. Each coin-filled sack weighed better than fifty pounds. He hung them two at a time across his saddle and led Patch back to his burial hole.

Once the sacks of coins were buried and the ground swept clear of tracks, he rode Patch back to the wagon one last time. He set a match to the hay in the wagon and rode off to the south once the wagon was ablaze.

Now, all I have to do is remember where I buried that plunder.

Sergeant Jones and his men had camped just outside of Mason while waiting for a reply to his telegram to Austin. Early the following morning, a boy rode into the Ranger campsite and delivered a telegraph message that instructed the Sergeant and his men to meet Major Jones in Fredericksburg as soon as possible.

The six Rangers rode into Fredericksburg just before dark. Major Jones and his escort were waiting for them in front of the Nimitz Hotel.

The Major said to all of the assembled Rangers, "Men, I want you to set up camp just west of town. I'll be out there first thing in the morning with fresh orders. Sergeant Jones, please come with me. I want to know what you found up on the San Saba."

After Sergeant Jones made his report, the Major said, "Keep this to yourself. Those wagons were carrying one hundred fifty thousand in gold coins destined for San Antonio. The Army plans to build a permanent base there to replace their temporary post. Someone must have learned of the gold and the probable route. Could you determine the direction that the wagons took?"

"Well, no, Sir. The Army showed up while we were scouting for sign and pritnear told us to skedaddle. Whoever killed them soldier boys and took their wagons did a pretty good job of rubbing out their tracks. I expect they used that old Injun trick of dragging brush behind them. Plus, that country is awful rocky and there are a lot of places where they wouldn't leave no tracks. But, if I had to guess, I reckon they headed south. They'd be liable to run into too many people if they went east, and the soldiers have that fort out to the west. If they were going to the north, why wait until the wagons got so far south? My money bets they went south."

Major Jones responded, "That sounds reasonable. I want you to take your men and return to Pegleg Crossing. Then, scout south looking for any sign of those wagons or their tracks. It is unlikely that they would follow the cattle drive trail since they would be seen. If I were doing it, I would parallel the drive trail out to the west a bit. Scour that country. My men will move west from here and then turn north to meet you. Meanwhile, I will go to San Antonio to see what the Army knows. You can contact me at the Menger Hotel."

Buck's trail through the brush took a sharp turn to the east and eventually opened out into a large open prairie. That night he made a dry camp and tended to his wounds. His abdomen and lower chest had taken on the purple-green coloration of a deep bruise. His leg was painful and swollen. He was running a bit of fever and felt light headed. He cut a big pad off of a prickly pear cactus and split it to expose the jelly like substance inside the pad. He smeared the jelly over the wound and tied his bandana back around his thigh. *That'll have to do until I can get to San Antonio.*

A week later, Buck rode into the south edge of San Antonio and stopped in front of a small house with a sign out front that said *Curandera.* An adolescent girl answered the door and led Buck into a small sitting room. An elderly woman who wore a long black dress and a heavy necklace made from some sort of animal vertebrae sat at a small table.

Buck asked, *"Hola Señora, usted habla inglés?"*

"Yes, enough. What may I do for you?"

Buck pointed to his thigh and said, "I have a small wound here and need some of your herbs to treat it. I have used the jelly from a *nopal* and it helped some, but I worry that it may become more serious as it does not heal even after a week."

The herbalist gave Buck a salve for the wound and a willow bark mixture that he was to use to make tea for his fever. He paid her and left for the city center.

Buck dismounted in the large plaza in front of the old, tumbled down mission that folks called the Alamo. He bought a bowl of a spicy red stew from a woman who had a sort of kitchen on a cart. He sat on a stone bench in the shade of a big cottonwood tree and ate his stew. Someone behind him tapped his shoulder and tried to flip his hat off. Buck quickly turned and saw Johnny Wilkins, the young Ranger he had met on his first day at the camp in Kerrville.

"Why, Buck, you old dog. What are you doing here? You're lookin' a might gaunt. You reckon that pepper stew will fatten you up?"

"Johnny, are you still in the Rangers?"

"Yepper, I laid out a spell but following a mule plowin' rocky ground seemed sorta dull. So, I reenlisted. Right now, I'm part of Major Jones' escort. He's holed up over yonder at the Menger. You oughta go over and give him a howdy."

"Boy Howdy! This is a spot of luck which I've been short of lately. I need to see the Major pronto."

Buck returned the wooden bowl to the woman cooking behind her cart and hobbled along beside Johnny toward the hotel.

"You got a catch in your giddy up. What's that all about?"

Buck said, "A fellow shot me in the leg a week or so back and I'm still a bit gimpy. But, it'll mend."

Buck was ushered into the Major's hotel room. Major Jones sat at a desk reading a report of some sort. He looked up and said, "Sergeant McDougal, how goes the rustler hunt?"

"Sir," said Buck, "I've stumbled onto something that may be a whole lot more important than a bunch of stolen cattle. While I was trying to determine the identity of the big boss of the rustling, I found a couple of Army wagons loaded with gold coins. And..."

"You what!?!" exclaimed the Major. "My God, man, you have probably saved the future of the city of San Antonio! You can't know how many people are searching for that gold. Where is it?"

"Well, I got into a little shooting contest with the man who I think stole it. He got away, but I got the gold and buried it where nobody but me knows where it is."

"Do you know who the man is?"

"I'll know him for certain when I see him. He runs a big

ranch down on the border southwest of here. I think his name is Hartright."

"There is a bank here in San Antonio called the Higgins and Hartright Bank. I wonder if it could be the same Hartright? Let me finish up a few things here, Sergeant. Meet down in the lobby in an hour and we will pay a visit to that bank."

It was a walk of only a few blocks to the bank building. Buck and Major Jones were being followed by four more Rangers. Buck held open the door as the Major and other Rangers entered the bank. Buck stood behind them. He was mostly hidden from direct view by the tellers and the men seated at the rear of the room. One of the seated men stood and walked up to the low, polished-walnut railing that separated the rear of the bank from the lobby. The man stuck his hand over the railing and said, "Major Jones, I am Jeb Higgins, co-owner of this bank. How may I help you?"

Buck stepped from behind the group of Rangers and pointed at the other seated man. "That's him, Major."

The seated man pulled a revolver from his desk drawer and fired a wild shot at Buck. A fusillade of shots from the Rangers cut the man down.

A woman who was at one of the teller windows screamed as she ran from the bank, "Robbers! Robbers! They've killed Mr. Hartright and are holding up the bank!"

Major Jones said, "One of you men go out and calm that woman down before we have a blood bath in here. It is bad enough that we have just killed the main suspect in the Army massacre on the San Saba."

XXXVII

A week after the shooting at the bank, Buck led a Cavalry detachment to the spot where he had buried the gold. He had left them while they were loading the sacks of coins into a wagon. He had mustered out of the Rangers with the blessing of Major Jones and a letter of commendation signed by both the Adjutant General and the Governor.

He sat by his campfire on the north bank of the Trinity River and reread the short letter from Becky.

Dearest Buck,

We need you here. We have thieves and rough men raiding us from below the river. Luke's store has been plundered and Luke seriously injured. With no local lawmen we are at the mercy of the worst men in Texas. Hurry home as soon as you can. I can write no more now.

Love,
Becky

★★★

Three days later Buck hitched Patch to the picket fence in front of Luke's house. It was well after dark but lights shone from the front windows. Buck climbed the four steps up onto the porch and rapped on the door. He said in a loud voice, "Hello, the house. It's Buck. Please let me in."

The door flew open and Luke's girlfriend, Sarah, grabbed Buck by the hand and led him into the parlor. She held her forefinger to her lips and whispered, "Quiet, Luke is sleeping. We've all been taking turns sitting with him."

Buck saw a shotgun propped next to the door and a revolver on the table. "Are you expecting trouble?" he asked.

"Well, Luke can identify the man who shot him, and we figured those outlaws might come back to finish the job. Papa's in the kitchen fixing a pot of coffee. I'll go fetch him."

Mr. Dobbs followed his daughter into the parlor. "Hello, Buck, it is very good to see you. You are well, I hope?"

"Yes, Sir, I'm okay but how is Luke?"

"Doc Pryor says he will survive but his recovery will be slow. He was shot through his chest and his right lung was hit. He lost a lot of blood but thankfully he is young and strong. Right now, we are praying that pneumonia does not set in."

"Can I see him? Is he able to talk?"

"He is asleep now. The doctor left laudanum for his pain. I gave him a heavy dose an hour ago. You can peek in on him but wait until morning to speak to him."

Buck asked, "Who is running Luke's store? Can I help with that until he recovers, or is there anything else I can do?"

"Becky Griffin and her friends have been taking turns at the store, but I worry that the outlaws may return. Becky saw the men who robbed the store and shot poor Luke. I fear for her safety as well but she says that she has a revolver and knows how to use it. Still, I worry for her and the other youngsters who are helping with the store."

"I need to see to my horse. I'll lay my bedroll out on the porch and spend the night out there. I am a light sleeper, and I reckon that Luke's dogs will set up a ruckus if anyone comes creeping up in the dark."

Buck was up just before sunrise. He had fed Patch some grain and turned him out into the pasture behind Luke's barn. As he stepped up onto the front porch, he heard a rattle of the fire grate on the kitchen stove. *I reckon someone is awake and rustlin' up some breakfast. I'll go see if I can help.*

Sarah was shoveling ashes out of the stove into an ash bucket. She looked up and gave Buck a smile. "We're so glad that you're here, Buck. We were worried sick that you had been killed by somebody down there in Texas. The stories we hear are dreadful. Are there any good people in Texas?"

"Yes, most folks in Texas are honest and friendly. In fact the name 'Texas' is said to come from an Indian word for friendly. Sadly, since the War Between the States, Texas has gotten more than its fair share of outlaws and renegades. And, like everywhere, there are homegrown crooks as well. In fact, my last job as a Texas Ranger wound up dealing with a crooked banker and a gang of local rustlers. But, enough of that. Let me get a fire going in that stove for you. What have you been feeding Luke?"

"Mostly just broth, but yesterday Momma got him to eat a little bit of scrambled egg. I'll try some more of that this morning along with broth."

After the stove was hot and Sarah was busy fixing breakfast, Buck went into Luke's room to check on him. Luke opened his eyes and gave a hoarse whisper, "Buck, when did you get here?"

"I rode in last night, cousin. Everyone says that you are recovering nicely and will be up and about soon. Sarah's in the kitchen working up some breakfast. The more you can manage to eat, the quicker you'll get your strength back. I've mustered out of the Rangers and am here to stay. I'll run your store for you until you are ready to take over. Anything you need, you let Ol' Buck know and I'll fetch it *muy pronto*. Lie back while I go see if your woman has your vittles ready."

After breakfast, Sarah said, "Buck, Can you help me change the dressing on Luke's wounds? I could go get Papa but you're right here."

"Why, of course, I'll help you. What are you putting on the wounds? An old Mexican lady down in San Antonio sold me some salve that I used on a bullet wound in my leg and the stuff was like magic. I've still got a little jar of it in my saddlebags. What say we put a dab of that on Luke's wounds?"

"I'm ready to try anything if you think it will help. Wait! What do you mean bullet wound in your leg?"

"It's a long story that I'll tell you all one day when we are all sitting by a fire with nothing to do but tell stories. Aren't you tired? Who is coming to spell you?"

"Becky will be over here once she gets someone set up to tend the store. She will be thrilled that you are here."

"Why don't I go over and run the store. You know that I ran it with Luke and James and Grandfather for several years."

After helping tend to Luke's wounds, Buck walked across the red dirt road from the house to the store. A mockingbird was fussing as she guarded the berries on a yaupon bush growing beside the store. A mockingbird and a flock of cedar waxwings were vying for possession.

The door to the store was locked, so Buck sat down on the bench on the porch and watched the antics of the birds. In a little while, he heard a buggy clattering around a bend in the road. It was approaching from the direction of the Griffin's farm. Buck expected that Becky would be driving. He leaned back and pulled his hat down to mostly cover his face and pretended to be asleep.

He almost coughed as the red dust poured over him. The buggy had stopped in front of the store. Then, he heard the click of a revolver being cocked.

"Keep your hands where I can see them, Mister. Any sudden move and I'll shoot you," said a young female voice.

Buck raised his hands to shoulder height and said, "Ma'am, you wouldn't shoot poor Ol' Buck, now would you?"

Becky let out a squeal. "Buck, is that really you? Laws, but I've missed you."

"Well, uncock your cannon and climb off that buggy."

After kissing and hugging for a few minutes, Buck said,

"I'll run the store until Luke recovers. You can go on over to the house and spell Sarah. She looks like she is about to drop from exhaustion. I'll tend to your horse and buggy. After she has gone home and Luke is sleeping, slip back over here and tell me what you can about the men who shot him."

"I can do better than that. Here's the key to the store. Look under the counter where Luke keeps his ledger. I've drawn pictures of the men and put them inside the ledger. I'll be back over here in an hour or so."

Jake said, "Lem, I'd shoot that horse if I was you. He's skittish, and you can't stay on him worth nuthin'. If'n you had a better mount or learned how to ride, we woulda caught that Injun gal afore she made it to that store. She come bilin' out the door with that scattergun madder that a red wasp. She woulda shot us sure if'n we had been closer. I reckon we'd best slip back up yonder one of these days and see if'n we kilt that Injun storekeep."

"Hell, Jake, you shot him near to plumb center. O' course, he's kilt. At least he had more money in the till than that storekeep over to Durant Station. How much did you say it were?"

"Never mind about that. We done drunk it all up on likker and are back flat broke. What say we mosey back up to Durant Station? That place was easy pickin's last time and maybeso they got a little more money in the till this time."

XXXVIII

Luke's recovery was slow. As he gained strength, he insisted on getting back over to his store. He settled into a chair that Buck had placed behind the counter.

Buck said, "Don't you trust me to run your store for you? I ain't going to steal anything, cousin."

"Of course, I trust you, Buck. It's just that I need to get out of that house for a spell. Sarah is hovering over my every move. And, any time I make the least little cough or groan, she rushes over like I'm fixin' to die on her. By the way, has anybody told you that we are set to be married next month? We had set the date before all this mess started."

"As a matter of fact, Becky did mention it. And, keep this under your hat, but I plan to ask Becky to marry me real soon. I just need to find the right moment."

A farm wagon rumbled up to the front of the store. After a few minutes, Mr. Griffin walked in. "Hey, Luke, you're looking better. Buck, do you have that order ready for me yet?"

"Yes, Mr. Griffin. Why don't you visit with Luke and I'll load it into your wagon."

"Before you get to that, I have news from over in town. It seems those same two outlaws robbed Mr. DuRant's store again. I would not be surprised if they showed up over here before too long. I've talked with some of the others, and we think we ought to put together a group to ride down there to Texas and clean out that mess. We'd like for you to join us since you are a former lawman. Johnny Wilson used to be town marshal over in Durant Station. He'll be riding with us."

"With all respect, Sir, if a bunch of you ride down into

Texas, you will likely start a little war. You certainly know how most Texans feel about Indians. Most of your group will be Choctaws. I wrote a letter to Major Jones, the head of the Texas Rangers, telling him about our problems up here. I received a reply just yesterday that temporarily reinstates me into the Rangers to deal specifically with these outlaws. Get your group to wait and see if I can get some justice done legally. I just need for some of you to help Luke with the store while I go down there and arrest these two owl hoots."

"Okay, Buck, do you want any of us to go with you?'

"No, it is better if I do this on my own. Your daughter has drawn what appears to be good likenesses of the men. Just give me some time."

Buck rode into the little town of Denison, Texas just after noon and found a crowd gathered outside the Marshal's Office. He tied Patch to a hitching rail in front of a store across the street and worked his way through the crowd up to the door of the office.

A deputy blocked his way and said, "Hold up, pardner. Nobody gets in here without Marshal Jinkins says so."

Buck pulled back his vest to display the badge pinned to his shirt. All he said was, "Texas Ranger, son." He pushed past the deputy and entered the office.

Buck held up Becky's drawings and said, "Marshal, I'm Ranger Buck McDougal and I'm looking for these two men. Can you tell me where I can find them?"

Marshal Jinkins looked at the drawings that Buck handed him. He looked up and grinned. "Yes, Ranger, I do believe I can tell you where these two are located. They're in a jail cell right through that door. I'm afraid that you can't have them. They killed two of our citizens, and we will be hanging them at noon tomorrow. You are welcome to stay for the execution if you like."

"Well, that saves me a peck of trouble. I'll stay to see

justice done. I'd just as soon see them hang for your problems as to have to haul them off to be strung up elsewhere."

Buck whistled to himself as he and Patch splayed though the tomato red water of the Red River. He had seen the hanging done and slipped his badge into his pocket. He was heading north toward home – at least the only home he had known since the farm back in Tennessee. *Home, I kinda like the sound of that but I reckon I need to build me ... us ... a house somewhere. Well, we'll sort that out together.*

San Saba Gold

EPILOGUE

The double wedding was held at the local church. Luke and Sarah were now settled into Luke's house. He still was a bit short of breath but had otherwise recovered. Luke and Sarah now ran the store together. He worked the counter and filled orders while she kept the books.

Buck had received a fifteen hundred dollar reward from the federal government for the recovery of the gold. He used some of it to buy a little farm on the edge of Durant Station. Buck and Becky's house was adequate although small. He was appointed Town Marshal in Durant Station where he served for twenty years. He and Becky had four children -- three girls and a boy.

In 1907 when Oklahoma achieved statehood, Caleb 'Buck' McDougal was elected to serve in the new state legislature.

www.ingramcontent.com/pod-product-compliance
Lightning Source LLC
Chambersburg PA
CBHW072351190626
46811CB00019B/502